Mr. JULY

Michele Dunaway

Dedication

For all of the firefighters who keep us safe

Prologue

The sun wasn't supposed to be shining on days like this. Rain would have been better—big, dark and stormy rain clouds would at least have matched Brad's anger and ire. Hard-slapping raindrops would also hide any slip of emotion, although men stoic in their Navy dress blues didn't shed tears. Yet the fight to hold them back was one of the hardest-fought battles of his life. A seagull took flight, finding his friends so they could play on the warm ocean breeze that blew across Coronado and made its way gently across the bay to San Diego. The breeze made the mid-eighties day perfectly palatable. Already Todd's elderly parents had been waiting over forty minutes for the Navy chaplain to begin the service, but Father Joseph couldn't begin until the casket arrived.

That was still a hundred yards away, being slowly carried along the assigned route.

Brad stood at attention, sweating under the dark

uniform that locked in the heat. He waited at the end of the line, the pallbearers made up of the current members of Todd's SEAL team, a role Brad had forfeited when he'd turned down the promotion. Brad had opted out of the transfer, and once his six-year enlistment ended, he'd head back to St. Louis. Todd had signed back up without any hesitation or backward glances. There'd been no talking him out of staying a SEAL. Less than a year later, his best friend was dead.

Brad could still remember the conversation when he'd told his friend—both he and Todd at a local dive, sharing a pitcher of beer over several games of pool. Todd was between overseas deployments, training for the mission ahead.

"You were finally going to be on my team. The guys and I were ready for it." Todd had taken a deep drink of the sudsy draft. Brad could still picture how he'd had to wipe his lip of the foam.

"Couldn't do it," Brad admitted. "I wish you'd followed me out."

"Thought about it. But I'm not cut out for civilian life. My country needs me."

"Scarlett needs you. She loves you."

"Yeah. But trust me, she understands." Todd drank more beer. Turned serious. "I need you to do me a solid. A favor. I'm shipping out in a few weeks."

On the same mission Brad would also have been on, had he chosen to say yes. "Anything, man. What are friends for?"

"Good. I know I can trust you. You've always had my back. Got a letter. For Scarlett. Should something happen.

Gonna snail mail it to you. I hope you'll never need it, but if you do, give it to her when the time's right."

Scarlett. Todd's wife. Brad's secret high school crush. But once Todd had called dibs, that had been that. Brad had stood as best man at Todd and Scarlett's wedding. Tried to forget how he felt about her. Told himself that thinking he was in love with her was nothing but a stupid obsession. A weakness to overcome. Something that would change when he found "the one." Only the one had never shown up, and his feelings hadn't changed. No woman compared.

The breeze shifted and Brad ignored the discomfort of standing at attention this long. On missions, he'd sat quiet and still for hours, but this was different, and the pain was wearing him down. He'd received the package a few weeks after that night in the bar, and inside was a sealed envelope addressed to Scarlett, along with some handwritten, one-page notes addressed to Brad upon which Todd had scrawled his last wishes—detailed instructions that Brad would now follow with military precision. In a twist of irony, today would be his last day in uniform. Tomorrow he'd fly back to his base, pack his things, and move home.

The honor guard carrying the casket came into sight. Behind, Scarlett walked, her certain step and emotionless expression designed to hide her grief. Brad could hear the thumps now, the sound of metal hitting the top of the casket as each of Todd's naval brethren removed his trident and set the metal badge atop the casket. The rhythmic thumping got louder as the casket came closer. "There's Mommy," he heard Todd's two-year-old daughter say. She was too young to fully understand what was going on and too small to walk the distance. "Shh," Todd's mother soothed, holding Colleen tight.

Brad straightened further as the trident-covered casket came within his reach. The pallbearers slowed, and with a thump, Brad added his own trident. Then they went past and up onto the dais, where dignitaries waited to honor the life of a SEAL gone too soon, but one whose heroic actions had saved the lives in his unit. Like precision clockwork, everyone moved into place and the service started.

Brad had seen Scarlett briefly last night after he'd flown in. Todd's parents wanted him buried in St. Louis, but Scarlett had relayed those weren't his wishes. Instead, inside the rental casket was an urn containing his ashes. Brad's gaze caught hers, and he shot the full force of his sympathy toward her. She was a proud woman, Todd had warned in the missives he'd sent. She would resist all outside help. But Todd had given Brad a job. Thought his best friend could somehow succeed in helping when all others failed, as Todd clearly believed they would.

Brad stared at the casket, at Todd's weeping parents, and at the drained, sad face of Todd's wife. Scarlett. No amount of telling her he was sorry would help now. He might be leaving the Navy, but he had to complete this last mission as assigned.

He owed it to his friend.

He owed it to his friend's daughter.

And he especially owed it to Scarlett.

The fact they were here today was entirely his fault.

Chapter One

The truth was, despite what all the songs said, including that one by Bon Jovi that really stuck in your head, you really couldn't go home again. Certainly, you could drive down the same streets. However, because time had marched on, nothing was exactly the same. Old buildings were torn down, replaced with something new. Others were repainted. Reroofed. Even that same road had been widened. Potholes filled. Stoplights stood where stop signs once sufficed. Some shops closed and others took their place.

As Scarlett Harrison exited Highway 44 (pronounced farty-farty by the locals), she turned right and drove her aged Prius down Grand. She hadn't returned to St. Louis in ten years, and found the trees along the Compton Reservoir barren, the park silent except for the one random jogger who braved the February midday chill and one homeless man who sat on a park bench wrapped in a threadbare blanket, his plastic bag of possessions by his feet. She moved into the far left lane, already missing California and its sunshine and warmth. The groundhog had clearly seen his shadow yesterday, for winter didn't want to give up its fervent grip on the Midwest. Thankfully St. Louis hadn't been hit like Boston, with record snowfall.

Victor Street—wasn't that name positively ironic— marked the end of her eighteen-hundred-mile journey, one she'd driven over the last four days. She'd closed on her and Todd's starter house the last day of January, and taken off, staying in a hotel three nights as she plodded her way back across the country. She'd tried to make it fun for Colleen, making sure they saw some of America's greatest wonders on the way, like the Grand Canyon.

Scarlett's journey had really started approximately two years ago, when the two uniformed Naval officers had shown up unannounced on her doorstep. She'd fallen to the concrete stoop, her hands clutching the metal railing. They didn't need to utter a word; she'd known why they'd come, and known what they would tell her would forever change her life.

Next came the funeral support team, and those men had become her navigators through the myriad of overwhelming arrangements. They'd stayed with her throughout the military service for her husband, who'd been her high school sweetheart. The only man she'd ever dated or loved. Oh, she'd tried to be strong. She'd tried to hold everything together, especially for her daughter Colleen's sake. Her parents had flown out. Todd's parents had flown out. She'd slept in the funeral home next to the flag-covered coffin, refusing to leave, even though all that was inside was an urn containing his ashes. She'd stood silent, sobs exhausted, as the honor guard folded that same flag into a tight triangle and placed it in her trembling hands. Later, after everyone had left the service, all she'd had left of her marriage was a flag and an urn. Her husband. Her future. Reduced to this.

She sighed and drummed her fingers on the steering wheel in a poor attempt to keep in sync with the radio. On Todd's final mission, his actions had saved sixteen people, although she knew little more than that, whatever it had been was still classified. But top military brass had shaken her hand. Told her Todd was a hero. Hundreds had shown up to pay their respects. He'd sacrificed himself, they'd said, and she had the commendations he'd never see to prove his heroism. Those medals, along with that same American flag, rode with her luggage in the back, underneath the protective trunk cover that hid the contents out of sight. Yet they were little comfort.

Not even on Grand a minute or two, and immediately before she reached Tower Grove Park, she made a left onto Shenandoah, an immediate right on Arkansas one block down, and then another hard right into the alley directly before Victor. The house that Brad owned was a few down from the corner, although because of all the garages lining the narrow one-way alley, all she could see were rooflines. The last time she'd seen Brad was at Todd' service. They'd known each other since high school, making it logical that

Brad was best man at her and Todd's Vegas wedding, one month after high school graduation and right before both men had shipped out to the Navy for basic training.

Later, both had gone through BUD/S together, but afterward had parted ways—Brad to one SEAL team, and Todd to another. Brad had done one enlistment and decided not to reenlist, making him ineligible for the transfer that would have sent him to Todd's unit, considered one of the Navy's finest. Todd told her he'd really thought Brad would reenlist early, like he had. That he looked forward to their working together. She knew Todd had been accepting of Brad's decision to opt out, but that he'd also been severely disappointed.

"Mommy? Are we there yet?"

"Almost," Scarlett called back to her four-year-old daughter. Seat belted into her booster, Colleen had been a trouper the entire trip, which had for the most part meant watching endless movies on the DVR-and-TV combo looped over the passenger seat, or by taking long naps, or by stretching her legs by climbing in fast-food restaurant playlands during their forty-five-minute pit stops.

Scarlett glanced in the rearview mirror. Colleen hugged her doll and craned her neck so she could peer out the window. Blonde hair like her mother's had escaped her pigtails. "Will my bed be there by now?" her daughter asked.

"Yes. Granny and Grandpa said the truck arrived yesterday and everything is already unpacked." Well, everything but the boxes. Those she'd do herself. "So your bed should be ready."

Colleen had inherited Scarlett's eyes and those pale green orbs widened. "Mommy, are those snowflakes? Will I get to see snow? Maybe play in it?"

"Yes, they are and yes, you will," Scarlett confirmed, managing a smile as a few flurries fluttered by. To a child, a first snowfall was special. Exciting. Magical. For an adult, it meant she and Colleen had gotten lucky. Despite the sky being a grisly gray for the last four hundred miles, the third day of February snow had held off, but by tomorrow St. Louis was expecting a good three to six inches. They'd arrived just in time. She shivered despite the heater running full blast. Time to go.

She pressed the power button, shutting down the car in front of the doors to an oversized two-car garage with living quarters on top.

"Is this our house?" Colleen asked. "And can I unclip?"

"You may unclip," Scarlett corrected as her daughter released the seat belt. "We have to go through the yard for our house. Brad lives above the garage."

"Brad, whose house we are renting," Colleen said, her statement designed to elicit her mom's confirmation.

"Yes. He and your daddy were good friends. Remember? I showed you the picture of them?"

Colleen nodded. "They were wearing a blue uniform."

"Yes. They were in the Navy together."

"Daddy and Brad were handsome. Winnie thought so too." Winnie was an American Girl doll and Colleen's constant companion. Todd's parents had sent it last

Christmas.

"Definitely," Scarlett agreed.

They'd been gorgeous men, even back in high school. When many male freshmen went through an awkward, geeky phase, both Brad and Todd had skipped it. Todd had been the heartthrob boy. His hair that one rare shade of ginger, worn loose and shaggy, that had made all the girls swoon. Blue eyes that had twinkled mischievously. His wide grin that went for miles had made her feel totally safe and loved. When his hair had been buzzed for the military, all the cut had done was accentuate high cheekbones and make him even sexier. Add a uniform and ooh la la. She'd been proud to be seen on his arm, especially at that one military ball they'd attended.

Then there was Brad. Whereas Todd was Mr. Happy-go-lucky, Brad had always been Mr. Serious. He'd been taller with darker hair the color of milk chocolate. His deep brown eyes had held an underlying intensity every time he gazed at her. He had an edge to him, as if he channeled the bad boy all mothers warned their daughters about.

She'd been attracted to him back in freshman year, even before she really understood what all those burgeoning feelings meant. His long glances sent her direction had made her lose her breath and feel things she hadn't felt before. She'd felt wild and silly at the same time. The connection between them had got the best of her one day when Brad had kissed her beneath the school staircase, hours before Todd had asked her out.

She pressed the pads of her first two fingers to her lips.

Thought back, but the front-end details were fuzzy. She knew she'd dropped her math textbook, and they'd knocked heads as both had reached for it. She'd seen stars, and he'd held her close to steady her, and then kissed her. Had her toes tingled? What she did remember clearly was that something had flashed in his eyes, and then he'd pulled away and left her standing there. Two hours later Todd had called and asked her out. She'd always liked Todd—who hadn't? He was easygoing and made her laugh, but with her lips still tingling from the kiss beneath the stairs, she'd asked Todd one question before she'd said yes: "What does Brad think?" Todd had answered, "He thinks my dating you is a great idea."

And that had been that. The kiss became an irrelevant secret—a momentary aberration. Something never spoken of again. Oh, she'd caught Brad staring at her every now and then with that same direct intensity as before, but he'd never been anything but friendly, as if the kiss had been something she'd imagined.

"Mommy?" Colleen caught her mom's gaze through the mirror. The seat belt snapped back into place after being released, and the whooshing noise jolted Scarlett into the present and out of her reverie. "I need to go potty."

"Me too." Scarlett climbed out, opened the back door and lifted her daughter from the car seat. Carried her through the wooden privacy fence gate, down a short brick path and up the steps to a small covered porch, where she set her down.

"I could have walked, Mom. I'm a big girl now,"

Colleen told her.

"This was faster." Scarlett set her down and lifted the mat, retrieving the key that had been placed there earlier this morning before Brad had left for a twenty-four-hour shift with the St. Louis Fire Department. She unlocked the door. Stepped inside. Gasped. The place was huge. Immaculate. Way beyond her price range with what little the annuity paid out each month.

Scarlett jolted her mom back to attention. "Potty, Mommy."

"This way." She quickly located the half bath just off a white, custom kitchen that looked like a picture in *Architectural Digest*. Got her daughter on the toilet in the nick of time. Held her up afterward so she could wash her hands in a custom marble sink with designer brass fixtures. They'd have to get a stool, she noted.

"It's big," Colleen commented, glancing around as they reentered the kitchen. "Is this a castle?"

"No," Scarlett replied, although the place felt like it. "It's just a historic house. That means it's old."

Colleen reached up and touched the lower stainless steel wall oven. "Everything's shiny. It doesn't look old."

Scarlett had to agree. Back in San Diego, the house she'd finally sold had aging vinyl floors, slightly yellowing white appliances and linoleum countertops that had seen far better days. Here the kitchen boasted speckled gray-and-white granite counters. Shiny eighteen-inch darker gray travertine tile covered the floor. A ten-by-six-foot granite countertop topped a huge kitchen island. There were two stainless steel wall ovens. A deep three-part sink with one of those tall, hose faucets. A six-burner Viking gas stove. "No, I guess this kitchen doesn't look old at all."

"So maybe it's a castle."

"Why not?" Scarlett agreed, trying to hide the fact she was overwhelmed. Brad had told her she could live rent free as long as she wanted, but she'd never planned on living off his generosity for more than six months at the most. There was no way she could ever afford this. However, since Colleen loved Disney princesses, she'd play along. "Brad told me there's a third floor and lots of stairs."

"So it's our castle?"

Scarlett hesitated, but answered honestly. "Yes." No need to tell Colleen they'd eventually have to move.

Colleen danced her way through the kitchen. "I always wanted to live in a castle. Can we get a kitten? I want a kitten to live with us in our castle."

"I don't know about the kitten just yet," Scarlett hedged, "but we can go explore our new home."

"Okay. But don't forget to ask Brad about the kitten."

They left the kitchen, entered an empty dining room with a beautiful chandelier. Underneath, on gleaming hardwood floors, sat her pathetic excuse for a kitchen table—as if a street ruffian had been let into a ball. Scarlett felt as out of place as her table looked. The sliding glass doors to the living room were open, making the two rooms almost seamless. "Look, Mommy! A fireplace!"

"I see." Scarlett walked through the doorway. She touched the ornate wooden mantel that surrounded the custom, inlaid tile that wrapped around the fireplace.

"I wonder if it works?"

"We'll have to ask Brad." She added that to her mental list. During one of their conversations, he'd mentioned he was rehabbing a house and needed someone to stay in it for a while. She hadn't been expecting this—Google hadn't done an updated street view here.

Colleen started twirling—the only thing in the living room a floor lamp. "It's like our own dance studio. Look at me go!"

As Colleen made herself dizzy, Scarlett wondered where the rest of her stuff was.

Colleen regained equilibrium, the large, happy smile on her face one Scarlett hadn't seen in a while. Her daughter tugged on Scarlett's arm, already done with the first floor and ready for her next adventure. Except for the small foyer, there were really only three big rooms on this floor, all with twelve-foot ceilings and a multitude of high, thin windows. The side windows looked directly at the brick wall of the neighbor's house, which was no more than ten feet away. "I want to see my bed."

"This way," Scarlett said, heading to the front staircase. This, too, was wood, all re-polished and re-stained. About seven stairs up, there was a small landing with a beautiful rose stained-glass window inset into the outside wall. They made the turn, climbed the rest of the stairs. At the top of the stairs a small hallway opened into a wide, center sitting room. Here they found their living room furniture and television. Toward the back of the house they discovered the rear staircase—which went down to the kitchen and up to the third floor—and a hall bathroom, a hall closet, and a bedroom, this one filled with the boxes containing their old life. Off the sitting room, toward the front of the house, was Colleen's bedroom, and Colleen found her bed and furniture already in place. The room had been painted a lovely shade of pale pink, proving Brad had listened to her when she'd described Colleen's room back in San Diego. A warm, fuzzy feeling washed over Scarlett. Brad had wanted to make Colleen feel welcome. Everything in the room matched perfectly.

Colleen bounced on her bed once. "Where's your room?"

"I guess the next one," Scarlett said, checking out her daughter's closet. Clothes were already hanging. Her parents, who'd told her they'd help unpack, had clearly concentrated their efforts on this floor, and Scarlett bit back the tears threatening to fall.

"Let's go find your bed. Maybe it's this way!" Colleen opened a door, which led into a large oversized bathroom with both a huge walk-in tiled shower and a huge claw-foot soaker tub. "Wow!"

Brad had clearly worked his magic; everything was new. The bathroom, done in Mediterranean blues and greens, felt like being at the beach. She'd only seen these types of bathrooms on those high-end real estate shows on HGTV. Real people did not have double sinks like that, or two shower heads.

Colleen pushed open another door. "Here's your

room! Look, the bathroom is a secret passageway."

"You're right." In their old house, they'd all shared one tiny hall bath. This en suite was bigger than her entire bedroom back in San Diego. The master bedroom here, with its ten-foot-tall windows overlooking Victor Street and its ornate fireplace, was larger than probably half her former house. Brad's house was a little overwhelming, and they hadn't even been on the third floor yet.

"Can I sleep in your bed tonight?" Colleen pointed to Scarlett's queen-sized bed, which, like the dining room table, seemed to be lost inside the massive space. "Just this once?"

"Of course, you can." Scarlett drew Colleen into her arms for a hug. Colleen hadn't slept well the past two nights, despite having gone swimming in the indoor hotel pool first. She was already a fish, much like her state champion father had been. Scarlett had to find more swimming lessons—stat.

"Good. Winnie and I would like to stay with you like we have in the hotels. And Winnie says thank you."

"Oh, she does?"

"Yes." Colleen tossed the doll onto the bed, which Scarlett's parents had made up. She'd call them in a few minutes. Let them know she'd arrived. Thank them for getting so many things ready. But what would she do with all this space? She didn't even have enough dishes to fill up the kitchen cabinets.

Not that the house wasn't beautiful. Having grown up in a tiny brick bungalow, she'd always fantasized about these beautiful old houses. Once, she and her mother had taken one of those house tours featuring inside peeks of the homes on Lindell, across from Forest Park. While this house was smaller than those, it was far too extravagant for two people. Yet now that she was here, she suddenly didn't want to leave. Wanted this beautiful dream home to be hers, despite knowing dreams were foolish follies.

"Are we getting our suitcases out of the car? Can we unpack?" Colleen tugged on her arm.

"Yes!" Scarlett said, shaking herself out of her doldrums. She missed the blue sky of San Diego, that was all. St. Louis winters were always multiple shades of one color: gray. "Of course we can get our stuff."

Scarlett carried the majority of the suitcases in two trips while Colleen carried her small one. They set them in the kitchen, and as they finished, the snowfall began to intensify. She allowed Colleen to stand on the back porch. Her daughter had never seen snow, and Colleen leaned over the railing and reached her hand out. "It's wet!" She tilted her head to the sky and stuck out her tongue. Laughed as she tried to catch the falling flakes.

"Okay, that's enough," Scarlett called. "The weatherman says there will be plenty of snow tomorrow."

Colleen got excited. "Will I get to build a snowman?"

Scarlett couldn't help but smile. "Yes. Granny brought one of cousin Eileen's old snowsuits for you, so tomorrow you can go out and play."

"Yay!" Colleen shivered. "I like snow."

"It is pretty," Scarlett admitted, for there was

something innately beautiful about fresh white powder. "But let's get inside since your jacket isn't warm enough to stay out here long."

"Okay. It's cold. Will it always be this cold?"

"No. St. Louis is only cold during the winter. In the summer it will be really hot."

"Like back home."

"Yes," Scarlett agreed, not correcting that this was their home now. She had to admit, snow and cold weather were two of the reasons she hadn't wanted to return. She'd delayed the inevitable as long as possible. First, she'd needed to wait until the real estate market had rebounded. She and Todd hadn't lived on the Navy base, and the house they'd bought and intended to fix up had never quite made it to the fixed stage. She'd managed to finally sell it to a rehabber and not be upside down. The proceeds from the sale had been enough to hire a moving truck to bring her possessions home, but that was about it. She didn't have enough for a down payment on her own place.

Oh, her parents had offered to help out and give her money. But she was thirty. It was time to be a big girl and solve her own problems. Besides, she'd wanted consistency for Colleen, and she'd wanted to grieve near her California friends. But slowly, those friendships had faded. Scarlett was no longer a military wife—she was a widow. A daily reminder that what happened to her husband could happen to her friends' husbands.

As the remaining life insurance ran out, she was glad she'd invested practically all of the initial payout into a trust fund for Colleen. Her daughter's college assured, Scarlett had realized that her future meant moving home to St. Louis. Hopefully two years had been enough time for Todd's family to grieve. Same for her own. She did not want either of them to see her return as a chance to meddle. As much as she missed Todd, this was her life. Her terms.

"Mommy, I'm hungry," Colleen announced, and Scarlett realized it had been hours since they'd eaten last, somewhere just east of Springfield.

"Granny said she'd stocked the fridge," Scarlett told her.

Colleen looked around the kitchen. "We don't have a refrigerator."

"Yes, we do," Scarlett said, finding it behind the cabinet doors. "See, it's built-in. And look, Granny filled it all up." Scarlett pulled out a pound of hamburger, then tried to figure out which cabinet would hold her frying pan. "Let me call Granny and I'll cook us something to eat. And then we'll unpack."

"Yay. Tell her we live in a castle. Can I help?"

Her daughter hadn't connected that her grandparents had already been in the house. "You may help," she agreed, not bothering to correct the grammar by repeating Colleen's question with the correct verb. "Go wash your hands again. Do you need me or can you reach?"

"I'll reach. I'll stand on my tippy toes."

As Colleen entered the bathroom, Scarlett began opening cabinets, scrounging for her frying pan. She found it in the last cabinet she checked, and called her parents once the burgers were sizzling.

"Hey, we're here."

"Good." She heard pure relief in her mom's voice. "The weatherman said it's about to get really ugly out there. I've been wanting to call you, but not if you were on the road."

"Well, we've arrived safe and sound. Thanks for the groceries. And for the unpacking. And for everything." Scarlett heard the slight tremble in her voice.

If her mom noticed, she pretended otherwise. "You're welcome, although Brad did most of it, including buying food. He's a good friend, that one. A good man. We can't wait to see you tomorrow. You use tonight to settle in."

"We will." Suddenly, Scarlett didn't feel like talking. Brad had helped? Hadn't he already done more than enough? When she'd pressed him a week ago as to why he was helping her, he'd brushed off her concerns. Evaded answering all her questions with a "Todd was my best friend." A wave of pure exhaustion rolled over her. "Hold on. Let me pass you to Colleen."

She passed Colleen her cell phone. "Hi, Granny! We're living in a castle," Colleen told her, and Scarlett could hear the excitement in her voice. "My room is pink. It's pretty."

Scarlett found a spatula and flipped the burgers. There were even buns and microwavable macaroni and cheese cups that just required you stir in some water. She pulled two of those out, ripped off the tops, got them ready to cook.

"Granny says she'll see us tomorrow," Colleen said,

holding out the phone.

"Mom?" Scarlett asked as she put the phone to her ear.

"You rest up tonight," her mom said. "And be sure to kiss my granddaughter for me. And honey, I love you. It's going to be great living here. You'll see."

After echoing, "I love you too," Scarlett set her cell down. She found plates, finished cooking. Tonight, like all the rest of the time on the road, the meal lacked vegetables. She'd worry about those tomorrow. Tonight, she just wanted to eat, cuddle with her daughter, and get some solid sleep. Much later, bath time skipped for this one night, both she and Colleen snuggled under the covers and fell fast asleep.

***

As Brad Silverman slipped into the churning current of the muddy Mississippi, he ignored the immediate shock caused by entering the frigid water. As a former Navy SEAL, Brad had been through much worse, both during BUD/S and during missions still too classified to talk about.

Today he fought the swift, ice-filled river for the St. Louis Fire Department's Marine Unit, searching for the man who'd fallen overboard. Unlike Brad, who wore a specially insulated wetsuit that covered every inch of his skin except his eyes—and those were covered with a specialty mask—the man exposed to this water would quickly succumb to the elements in five to seven minutes.

He prepared for the worst. Despite his gear, he could feel the cold seep into his bones. But he pushed through, hoping he'd be in time; he'd dealt with death too often and would prefer tonight not be one of those nights. He nodded to his partner, Lewis Graham, who was forty to Brad's newly minted thirty. Lew, half-human, half-fish, still competed in triathlons and always won his age group. Despite the rock-hard six-pack abs that Brad had exposed in that god-awful charity calendar he'd been talked into doing, Lew still made Brad, who swam ten miles a day, feel like a proby.

With the St. Louis Fire Department's Marine Unit Task Force for almost a year, Brad loved his job, especially the thrill and danger of saving people. After leaving the SEALs, he knew he needed a job that kept him active and even though he had to go through the fire academy, he knew he'd made the right choice. "I see him!" Brad called, and together he and Lew retrieved the man, the rescuers on the fireboat reeling in the ropes to pull them all to safety.

"I think he's alive," Brad heard someone call as the boat sped across the water. He and Lew leaned back, the subzero wind smacking against their faces. Firefighter paramedics worked on the man they'd rescued, and once on shore, they transferred him quickly to the waiting ambulance.

Forty minutes later, back at Station 11, where the task force called home, Brad held a mug of hot black coffee laced with five packs of sugar between his hands. His fingers were numb; the chill of the water hadn't worn off yet. Worse, the other quint truck had been out on a call, and a blast of cold air seeped into the living quarters as the huge doors opened when it returned home. Brad glanced at the clock. Eight thirty p.m. The sun had been down for almost three hours, and Scarlett should have arrived at the house. Carrying his coffee, Brad retrieved his cell phone from his locker. She'd sent him a brief text, telling him she and Colleen were home and going to bed.

He allowed himself one huge sigh of relief. Even though he'd helped her parents set up her furniture, part of him hadn't believed she'd really move. Every day he'd waited for her to call and tell him she wasn't coming, that she'd changed her mind, that she was staying in California.

Scarlett was stubborn, and for the past two years since Todd's death, Brad had watched as she'd refused everyone's help. He'd listened during their phone calls—ones he'd always initiated. Two years ago, he'd called her monthly and she'd only talked for a few minutes. Then their conversations had grown longer and longer, and he'd called her every other week, then talking weekly for about an hour each time as her other friends drifted away. At first the conversation had been one-sided, more him than her.

She'd fought the idea of moving back to St. Louis. She hadn't wanted to be dependent on anyone, especially her parents. He couldn't blame her. He understood independence. and who wouldn't miss the sun and surf, especially on days like today, when he went into an ice-packed river to perform one of the twenty-five to thirty river rescues the department did per year.

He sipped more coffee, and pulled the photo from where he kept it on the top shelf of his locker. There they were, *frozen* at their graduation. Todd on the left, then Scarlett, then Brad, wearing their robes. The ginger, the blonde and the brunette, his mom had called them. That day they'd vowed to be friends forever. Less than month later, he'd stood by Todd as he'd married Scarlett in a gaudy Vegas ceremony crammed in before they'd started basic training.

Brad reached into his locker, pulling out the manila envelope. He turned it over, studying creases long memorized. He knew the instructions inside by heart. Inside were two letters—one for him and one for Scarlett. Todd had given implicit directions as to when Scarlett's letter was to be delivered. Even though he was curious, Brad had never looked at her letter. A man did not question his orders and his best friend's last request. Whatever Todd had written, it was for Scarlett and for Scarlett's eyes alone.

A loud noise erupted as the loudspeaker blasted out another call.

Brad quickly put the photo and the envelope back. He closed the locker and put his coffee mug in a safe spot as he raced for his gear. When not out on the water with the task force, Brad was a firefighter, and he was headed to a house fire, probably another one started by a faulty space heater. They'd had three of those this month already, one with tragic results.

It's one reason he'd gutted his house and installed all

new, top-of-the-line, high-efficiency HVAC. Even with three floors, Scarlett and Colleen would be warm. Now that both were under his roof, he could finally fulfill the promises he'd made to Todd. He hoped so. Maybe then the guilt would stop.

Chapter Two

After sleeping like the dead, it was the strange noises that finally woke her. There was a scraping sound. Then a faint whoosh. She lay in bed with eyes partially opened in the darkened room and tried to place the sound. She sat up in bed as the ten-year-old memory returned. Scrape. Whoosh. Scrape. Whoosh.

Someone was shoveling the sidewalk. First came a gritty push of metal blade on concrete, followed by the whoosh of snow flying. The bedside clock flickered ten a.m., meaning she and Colleen had slept almost twelve hours. She consoled herself that it was only eight in San Diego. She slid out of bed, so not to disturb her daughter, pulled down the T-shirt that had crept up and headed to the front windows. She pushed aside the thick heavy curtain and looked down. At least five inches of snow covered the front porch roof. Beyond that she saw Brad at the end of the front sidewalk, where it formed a T with the sidewalk that ran parallel to the street. Sans hat, glossy dark hair gleamed in the midmorning sun.

Scrape. Whoosh. He lifted the light snow easily, and she saw him stop to wave at a neighbor across the street. The forty-something neighbor shook her head. Mouthed back she was fine. Brad returned to the walk, sending another shovelful flying. Although Scarlett couldn't see any arm muscles bulging under the bulky black parka he wore, he made the work appear effortless. The parka dropped over his hips, and she followed the line down a pair of faded blue jeans that tucked into heavy, mid-calf snow boots. The bad boy that sometimes haunted her dreams had turned domestic. Who would have thought? He attacked the walk with a concentrated gusto that hinted at a leashed power, one that if let loose . . . She trembled slightly. He'd never scared her, but he was dark and brooding in that Heathcliff sort of way, although even that description didn't quite fit.

One brief, stupid kiss and he'd been a watchful presence, a forbidden fantasy pushed to the far recesses of her mind.

Sensing her, he glanced up and caught her staring; she gave him a brief, guilty wave and then let the curtain drop into place. Colleen was now awake and sitting up in bed. "Get into the bathroom," Scarlett said. "And I bet your tummy is rumbly."

"I am hungry," Colleen agreed. Ten minutes later, with their teeth brushed and both of them dressed, they made their way down to the kitchen. She had no idea how to work the brand-new, work-of-art coffee machine, which was sitting on the counter, so instead she found the hot chocolate packets and a large measuring cup, which she filled with water and put in the microwave.

She retrieved a bowl from the third cabinet she opened. Finding the puffed rice cereal only took one try. Milk, well, that was easy. Spoons were found in the fourth drawer she pulled open. Colleen had climbed up onto one of the eight bar stools surrounding the island and pretty soon Scarlett had her daughter eating cereal and sipping hot chocolate. Scarlett used the remains of the hot water to make her own cup of hot chocolate. She heard the stomps on the back porch before she saw the shadow in the doorway. The bell buzzed and she unlocked the door to allow Brad to step inside.

"Hey," he said. "Good morning."

"Good morning to you, too," she said, taking a step back as he moved forward. At six feet, he towered over her smaller, five-five frame. This was the first time she had seen him since the service. If possible he'd gotten even better looking. The sharp angles and brooding stare that once gave him a bad boy vibe now made the man standing before her stunning. No gray marred his temples, his hair still a wild mess as dark hair swooped toward his left eye, fell in a wave and curled around the bottom edge of his ear. Sexy, night-before stubble graced his jawline, made a circle around full lips that drew a woman's attention immediately. Even her daughter stared at him, transfixed, as if a real life Disney prince had walked in their back door.

Brad was Prince Eric, Prince Charming and Snow White's prince all rolled into one.

He closed the door, shutting out the arctic blast and shoved GORE-TEX gloves into a parka pocket. His lips formed a tight kiss as he blew on his hands. "It's chilly out there."

"Mommy?" Colleen asked, green eyes still wide. "Who is this?"

Scarlett snapped to attention. Where were her manners? She waved Brad onward. "Come in, come in. Colleen, remember those pictures I showed you? This is Brad. Brad, Colleen."

"He's not in uniform." Her nose wrinkled as she studied him.

"Nope, I'm off today," Brad told her, leveling her with a high-wattage grin that had the power to thaw even the toughest of little girls and even smarter women.

Colleen melted immediately. "Is this your castle? I like it."

"Castle? What?" He turned confused brown eyes Scarlett's way. While he knew how to melt hearts of all ages, he clearly didn't know how to talk to little girls. Still, that gaze knew how to hook a woman.

"Colleen believes we live in a castle now. She's very into Disney princesses," Scarlett clarified. "Our old house was as big as this whole floor."

"It's a very big house," Colleen told Brad with an all-knowing nod. "So it must be a castle."

"Sure it is," Brad agreed, clever enough to play along.

"All you need is a prince."

"I'm still too young to marry a prince. Mommy says I need to be at least twenty and besides, they've all been taken. Mommy also said that no prince is going to find her because she was married to my daddy. Princesses are single until they find their one true love."

"I did not know that," Brad said, holding back a chuckle.

As Colleen went back to eating her cereal, Scarlett's face reddened and she made a beeline for the center island, putting Brad squarely on the opposite side. Out of the mouths of babes . . .

She gestured to her cup. "Would you like some hot cocoa?"

"It's good," Colleen added to her mom's offer. "But the marshmallows don't last long. We usually use whipped cream, but Granny forgot to bring that."

Brad peered into her cup. "You're right. I can see that the marshmallows are gone. I'll have to buy some whipped cream. I'll remember that next time." He smiled at her, directed his question to Scarlett. "Did you by any chance make coffee?"

She shook her head. Pointed to the shiny machine. "I have no idea how to use that thing."

"Here. I'll show you." He slid out of his parka, tossed it over the back of a kitchen chair. Underneath he wore a fisherman's knit sweater and tight jeans that did little to conceal. Were women crazy? Why hadn't someone put a ring on his finger? Todd had always told her Brad had had no issue meeting women. He opened a cabinet, took out some coffee beans. "Want one?"

She held up her mug. "I'm good."

"Sure? It's French roast." He showed her bag and gave her a megawatt grin that melted her insides. Made her suddenly want to find out what all those other women he'd dated had experienced. Seriously, she had to get a grip. It had been a long time since she'd felt the full effects of a man's smile. That was all.

"Already have cocoa." She sipped quickly, pushing aside the silly glow his attention had created.

The smile didn't diminish. "We can buy some of that. The machine makes it too. Does espressos, lattes. You name it. It's a commercial machine made for the kitchen"

"There's nothing wrong with the old-fashioned small ones. This thing is so fancy. Todd and I made the instant stuff." She winced. She sounded testy. No need for him to suspect the physical effect he was having on her. Had to simply be the stress from the move. Right?

He didn't appear to notice or take offense as he dumped the beans in and the machine ground them. "Where's the fun in that? It's time you had grown up coffee. I'll teach you, and then you can make it for yourself. And me. On occasion. If that's okay with you."

Something wicked and mischievous slipped into his eye, as if he were daring her. "Maybe. If you're lucky." But the words didn't come out as teasing and unaffected as she'd hoped.

"Then lesson one. Real coffee is worth the extra steps."

The machine began to hiss. Colleen set her spoon next to her bowl and wiped her lips with a paper towel. Surely their cloth napkins were somewhere, but Scarlett hadn't yet found them.

"Mommy, may I be excused?"

"Yes, but . . ." She had no idea what to do. The books were still packed. While Colleen's bed was assembled, most of her toys were still in boxes.

Brad sensed Scarlett's concern. "I hooked up the TV yesterday. Cable's already on. My mom also sent over some animated movies that Lisa's outgrown."

Lisa was Brad's niece. She was ten, and his sister Cynthia's child. Unlike Todd, who'd been an only child, Brad had three other siblings.

"Thank you," Scarlett said gratefully. "We're going to unpack her room first thing. Shall we see what's on TV? Or if maybe there's a princess movie in the bunch Brad's sister sent?"

"Okay." Colleen scrambled down from the bar stool. "I liked the Frozen movie too. Maybe that's there."

"Probably not, but we can look," Scarlett said, following Colleen up the back stairs. "Feel free to help yourself to anything. After all, you bought it all," she called over her shoulder.

Brad digested her parting words, wondering if there was hidden meaning as Scarlett disappeared from view, her bare feet climbing up the hardwood stairs he'd polished to a sheen himself and then she disappeared out of sight.

Even though he knew he'd been breathing the entire

time, he exhaled a breath as if he'd been holding one as if afraid of making a misstep. He ran a finger over a portion of the granite countertop, whose entire installation had needed the help of three of his firefighter buddies. Renovating this house had been an all-consuming project, something to fill every spare moment when not on the job.

Perhaps working on the house had helped him deal with any residual PTSD. Unlike Todd, he'd never been in the line of fire on a daily basis. He hadn't killed anyone. Didn't have blood on his hands, unless you counted Todd's. He knew he carried that guilt. He knew he'd been affected by both that and his time in the service. Death and he weren't friends. He'd seen far too much death as a SEAL, and as a firefighter, he still dealt with death, whether it was caused by car accidents, drug overdoses, heart attacks or smoke inhalation. Where you had life, you had death. That was an inevitable fact. Still, perhaps this house had saved him, for it had given him purpose.

That sounded a bit crazy, but he didn't care. These past two years he'd let his house become his mistress. It filled a void and gave him purpose. A man had to have purpose. Once after two pitchers of beer, Todd had admitted he didn't think he'd be able to adjust to civilian life—but somehow Brad had managed to do that. Maybe it had helped going directly into another adrenaline-junkie job, one that involved hard danger and risking your life saving people. Last night he'd pulled the young boy out from the building. While the house had been a total loss, all inside had survived the fire, including the family cat Brad had saved as well. He liked saving things. Better than the alternative.

Noticing a plantation blind was crooked in the breakfast nook, he went to adjust it. He then moved some small packing boxes on the table so he could set down the slightly chipped, blue ceramic coffee mug he'd found in the cabinet. Scarlett deserved nice things, not remnants. But Todd had never been good at money managing. He'd always figured he'd hit a jackpot tomorrow.

Brad shifted a stacked box and froze as he saw the flag. It was folded thirteen times so only white stars and blue fabric showed, the same as when the honor guard had handed it to Scarlett following the memorial service. She'd put it in a black display box made for such items. It rested on the table by her car keys and purse, as if she'd carried the items inside last night and set them down, perhaps intending to return to rehome them later.

Fingers shaking, he relocated the coffee cup to a more secure location, careful not to spill any of the coffee that threatened to slosh out. He returned to lift the brass latch and opened the glass. His finger touched the fabric that had covered his best friend's casket and he fought back the tears and anger that threatened. Todd shouldn't have died. Why hadn't Brad convinced Todd to follow him out? To be a better father and a husband?

And hell, could Brad really have changed things had he reenlisted and accepted the transfer into Todd's unit? He'd never know that answer, and Brad shoved guilty thoughts away as he heard Scarlett's feet reach the bottom stairs, for despite applying extra nails to the subfloor before the installing the new wood, the last step still gave a small squeak. "You okay?" she asked.

He closed the glass lid, his fingers fumbling as he secured the latch. "Fine." Even to his own ears, his voice sounded clipped, far away. He masked his expression and turned her way.

She pointed at the flag. "I have no idea where I'm going to put that. But I guess there's plenty of room." Her forced laugh sounded hollow. False. She waved a hand in an absent yet deliberate gesture. "This place is huge. I haven't even been on the third floor yet. Colleen's right. It's like a castle."

"I'm sorry." The words burst forth. Hung on the air like an oppressive summer day.

She planted hands on hips. Took a moment to study him before she made light to his darkness. "It's not your fault you rehabbed a three-story historic house. It's a beautiful place. We're fortunate you've invited us to stay here."

Her silent plea of "don't go there" was written from the top of her brow to the tip of her chin, and he'd never been one to be able to deny her anything—although in honesty, she'd never asked. So he got a grip on his emotions. Went along with the change in the conversation. "Thanks. Only a few more construction things left to do. You sure you won't mind if I'm in here finishing up? It's mostly work that needs to be done on that third floor you still haven't seen." To his ears, his chuckle sounded fake. Even he had to admit his attempt at a lame joke also fell flat.

However, clearly thankful he'd played along and not pushed his apology further, she smiled, and the result was it lit up her whole face. She'd always had the power to make him go weak at the knees. When he'd first met her, back in freshman English class, he'd noticed her smile. Sure, back then it had been covered with silver braces, but he'd liked how whenever she looked at him, that one simple action had tugged at something deep inside. Now years later, her smile still had that power to make his heart leap. Time still hadn't abated his feelings for her, which he'd kept totally hidden and would continue to do so. He was bound and determined his desire for her would not complicate things.

"Of course it's not a problem if you're here," Scarlett reassured. "After all, I'm your guest, and while we need to address that issue of rent down the road, because it's clear I'm not paying you enough—"

"We don't need to do so today," Brad interrupted.

"Fine. But since it's your place, all I ask is that you give me a bit of advance warning so Colleen and I are dressed. I guess that's the only ground rule. Like you did today, just knock. And maybe I'll learn to use this coffee machine."

"I will." He hesitated. "I won't be disturbing anything. As in . . ." He paused. How did he ask this?

She frowned. "What do you mean?"

He pointed to the flag. "Todd. His . . . his remains." He had no idea what she'd done with them. "Are they here? I don't want to knock them over."

Pale green eyes widened, as she understood. "You

mean his ashes."

"Yes. I don't want to accidently knock over the urn if I have to move things around." Brad wasn't sure if he could handle even seeing them. Once the service had been over, he'd left immediately. He'd made his excuses that he didn't have any more leave, especially with only a few more weeks on his enlistment. He'd known she was in good hands— her parents and Todd's were there. And there was nothing Brad could do. Not then.

Scarlett's lips quivered. She straightened. Found her fortitude. "No worries. I spread his ashes in the Pacific right before we left. Seemed fitting to finally let him go if we were coming here."

She paused as her voice cracked and Brad felt the emotion as if a knife plunged him in the heart as she touched the base of her throat. She coughed. "He loved the water, and you know as well as I did that he never wanted to come back here. That's why I didn't bury him in Jefferson Barracks. I know Larry and Louise were upset, for they thought he should be buried here. Thank goodness he wrote that down."

"They could be difficult."

"Yeah. But I wanted him to rest in peace on the waves, exactly like he wanted." She reached for her hot chocolate. Poured the tepid remains in the sink. Worked the fancy sprayer faucet that was the latest designer rage. "Does that sound silly? Was I wrong?"

"No. Not if he wanted that. His wishes should be respected. He wrote it down, as you said. He knew what he was doing if he wrote it down."

Like the letters he'd sent Brad. As a distraction, Brad reached for his mug. To control his nerves he'd taken a long sip of French roast that he'd sweetened with a bit of cream. The coffee had cooled slightly, but was still hot enough that it scalded the back of his throat

"I know Larry and Louise weren't please he never wanted a graveside service or a marker. We talked about it once, Todd and I. After he reenlisted. I remember laughing, trying to ease some of the heaviness of the moment. It was so serious, you know? He never planned for the future but for some reason he wanted to plan for this." Her words caught. "I mean, we were planning what happens if he died. Who laughs about something like that? But I did. I found it surreal."

"A normal person laughs because it's that or cry," Brad consoled. "Besides, Murphy's Law. You plan for it and then it doesn't happen. If you don't, it does."

"Or it becomes a self-fulfilling prophesy." She sighed and he watched her throat move. "It was one of the most awkward conversations of my life. Maybe it was his way of letting me know that he'd never leave the SEALs. That he was in the Navy for life, however short or long that life would be. He said whatever happened that he never wanted a tombstone, even if the Navy was buying. Told me I was to move on, not come back to see him yearly and bring him flowers or plant a flag on Memorial Day. Who says that?"

Her voice broke and filled with anguish. "Why didn't

he respect what I wanted? All Colleen has are pictures and mementoes. How do you talk to someone without a grave?"

"He must have had his reasons," Brad defended, totally in agreement with her. He'd told Todd that, but Todd did what he wanted, like he always had, leaving Brad to pick up the pieces. Once they'd built a wooden bench for a park as part of a Boy Scout project, and Todd had lost interest halfway through. Brad had finished it.

Scarlett gathered her composure. "I'm sure you're right. I shouldn't have dumped on you. Despite all of our phone conversations, we've only recently started opening up and becoming better friends and here I am, partial to your hospitality. I'm sorry. It won't happen again."

"It's okay. No apology necessary."

She took the flag and set it inside an open box. Folded the cardboard flaps over it. "Two years later you wouldn't think I'd be so frustrated."

Brad lifted his coffee mug to his lips, a deliberate evasion tactic. How did he respond to that truth? What he wanted to do was drag her into his arms and give her a huge hug. He should tell her that there was a letter. That Todd had thought of her and had things he wanted her to know. But Brad kept silent. As much as he cared for the woman standing in his kitchen and wanted to make everything better, he had to follow Todd's last wishes as outlined. The room muted as conversation ceased. The new windows he'd installed for the most part muffled the outside world. He'd added extra insulation between floors,

39

which meant that neither Scarlett nor he could really hear the television Colleen was watching.

She walked over to the seamless sink, made of high-end white granite composite, a look he'd liked better than stainless steel. She emptied Colleen's bowl. Ran the nearly silent disposal. Filled the void by saying, "Are you sure I can't get you anything to eat? I'm pretty good at cooking scrambled eggs. It's one of the few foods I've mastered."

He shook his head, suddenly itching to leave before he did anything stupid like cross the room and take her into his arms. "I'm fine. I've got more shoveling to do. I didn't mean to intrude; I just wanted to check in on you. Make sure you got settled okay."

"Yes. We made it without problems. It's a lovely house. I know I keep saying that but it's true." Her left hip rested against the beveled edge.

He'd bought it soon after moving home. "Glad you like it. It's been a labor of love., and I'm glad you're here. It's too big for me and the market hasn't yet recovered. And you won't mind me finishing, which is more than another tenant might say."

"I don't want to accept charity." Hands went to her hips. She'd always had a small waist, one his hands could encircle.

"We'll talk about it later. But think about this. How is it charity? You're doing me a favor. By you living here, you'll find any issues that the house might have. You know, cold water after five minutes, or if the toilet flushes during a shower. That type of thing."

She appeared skeptical. Her eyebrows wrinkled, as did her nose. "If you say so."

He folded his arms and dug in. He couldn't do what Todd asked him without her being close by "I do."

She didn't appear convinced. Shifted so her backside was against the edge of the sink. Waved a hand in a general indicator of the room—a similar motion to the one she'd made earlier on the stairs. "You have to admit this is . . . strange."

"How so?"

Her chin jutted forward. "Me being here. Living in your house. You kissed me once."

He wasn't going down this path, especially when she was right. "Yeah, in high school before you dated Todd. We were kids. You're making a bigger deal out of my generosity than it is. As I said, you're actually doing me a favor. That's all. So no worries. Let it go."

"Like the song?"

His forehead creased. "What?"

"Hmm, you haven't seen *Frozen*?"

"No clue what you're talking about."

"It's a kid's movie. It was all the rage. Colleen found it in the bin. She's watching it right now."

"Nope. Not into cartoons." He reached for his coat, tugged it on and pulled out his gloves. "Gotta get moving. I'll check on you later. See if you need things moved around."

He went to the door, and as he opened it, there stood Scarlett's mother and father. "Brad!" her mother enthused, standing on her tiptoes to kiss his cheek. "Leaving?"

The last thing he wanted to do was intrude on family time. "Have more snow to shovel and I really want to rest. Got off at eight this morning."

"You didn't sleep yet?" Scarlett asked, frowning.

"Got in a couple of hours at the firehouse," he evaded. "Catch you all later." He started to leave, then turned around and looked at her for a beat too long. Damn, he had to get a grip. "I really am glad you are here."

***

Brad's words had dropped an octave, and Scarlett could feel the energy between them as she watched Brad go down the back porch steps, shovel soon gripped in hand. She heard the scrape and whoosh come from somewhere behind the back porch before the door closed. The sound jostled her from the trance she was in. He was clearing the patio.

"I can't believe you're finally here!" Her mother, obviously oblivious to what just happened, drew Scarlett in for a huge hug, her quilted down parka cold against Scarlett's skin. "How was the drive? Long, I'm sure from your texts. Where's my beautiful granddaughter?"

"She's upstairs watching a movie," Scarlett said.

Her mother peeled off her coat, her boots dripping melted snow on the gray tile floor. "Mom, shoes," Scarlett admonished. Thank goodness Brad wasn't here to see the mess.

Her mom glanced down. "Oh, yes. I'll clean it in a minute. I'm just so excited. I can't believe I'm going to get to see Colleen every day. I've already scheduled her first Granny playdate. Oh, and we do need to talk preschools. Or at least a mother's-day-out program." Boots and coat were dropped in the middle of the floor as her mother called, "Colleen! Granny's here!" and headed up the backstairs.

Scarlett stared helplessly at her dad, who simply shrugged. "Sorry."

"She can't just take over now that I'm home," Scarlett said, retrieving her mom's things. She set the coat on a chair and the shoes on the doormat. Her father had grabbed a paper towel and was already wiping the floor. "Dad, I would have gotten that."

"It's no problem," her dad said, opening the cabinet she'd seen Brad open earlier, the one with the trash can. "Been cleaning up after your mom's enthusiasm for years. The things you do for love. But now that you're older, you're on your own with her."

"This is why I didn't want to come back."

"Sorry, kiddo. I know. But since here you are, my advice is that you'll need to set the boundaries and do it quickly. That's what your sister-in-law Maureen had to do. But be prepared for push back. You know how your mom is. But she'll fall in line. She loves you too much not to abide by your wishes."

"Good to know."

"Hey, Maureen has it down. Call her."

Maureen had been married to Scarlett's brother for eight years. Neither had flown out for the memorial service, but Scarlett hadn't expected her older brother to attend because Sean had been downsized several months before Todd's death—he and Maureen had three kids. Sean was working now, thankfully, and in reality, Scarlett would have done the same thing if every nickel counted. Heck, she was here living in Brad's house because money was tight and she'd been unable to continue making mortgage payments. Who knew she'd trade in that shack for a castle?

Temporary castle, she admonished herself. Despite Brad saying she could stay as long as she liked, she refused to take any charity for a minute longer than she needed. No matter how tempting this kitchen.

She could hear muted voices upstairs, and her father had gone back outside to the car. "Luckily Brad's car is in the garage, I'm parked next to you," he said, bringing in two armfuls of cloth grocery bags. He rubbed his feet three times on the mat. "Seeing that Brad bought you hamburger, your mom stocked up yesterday before the storm. She said it was crazy. People thinking they need milk and bread as if a few flakes are about to bring down the apocalypse. The roads out there are already clear."

"San Diego could get somewhat crazy if a massive rainstorm was coming in."

"Human nature to be prepared, I guess. Better than the alternative." He set the grocery bags on the massive island and straightened. Nearing sixty, her dad still stood at six feet two. His hair had turned white, and aside from the requisite wrinkles, he appeared in his prime. An avid cyclist, he hadn't added any of the weight of most middle-aged men.

Brad hadn't either, she realized. Despite the fisherman's sweater, she could still see he was as cut as ever. Or was the word ripped? She wasn't up on the current slang. He'd kept in top shape even after leaving the service. He'd always been built; Brad had been a three-season high school athlete: soccer goalie, baseball pitcher and swimming state champ. Todd hadn't been too shabby either. The Navy had hardened Todd up, and she assumed they'd done the same to Brad. The SEALs had formed Todd into a living Greek sculpture. Their senior year, Todd had been the lead-off leg for a 200 IM relay that Brad had anchored. Their team had set the state record for the event. Scarlett still had the gold medal, in a box with more of Todd's cherished mementoes. She'd put them away, saving them for Colleen.

Her mom returned, sans Colleen. She'd pulled the stocking cap off her head, making her hair frizz. She looked like a wild version of Mrs. Weasley from *Harry Potter*.

"I love this kitchen," her mom said. "Huge. Oh, good. The food's in." She reached for the bag. "I bought you pork chops and . . ." Her voice trailed off, thought derailed, as she began to load everything into its place. Scarlett busied herself with opening drawers. While part of her was grateful the heavy lifting of moving was finished, she liked to organize her kitchen herself. Put items where she wanted them.

As it was already done, probably no point in moving things around now. Easier to learn where everything was.

Her mom pulled out a canister of hot cocoa powder, the kind that needed to be measured. "Figured you could try to make this in that fancy machine over there. Colleen still loves hot chocolate, right?"

"She had some instant this morning. We were only missing the whipped cream."

"And I remembered that." Her mom pulled out a red-and-white can with a red plastic cap. "Hot cocoa's always better with whipped cream. Oh, and remember, you need to shop at Schnucks over on Arsenal. It's the best grocery store in this area. I don't like the one farther south on Grand."

"I'll keep that in mind," Scarlett said.

"I looked up your address and you're in St. Pius," her mother said as she stowed the last of the groceries.

"I hadn't checked." Organized religion wasn't high on Scarlett's list of priorities.

"The boundary is Shenandoah, so you squeaked in by literally a block. So you'll be in our parish."

"That's great," Scarlett offered with little enthusiasm. She could already picture her leisurely Sunday mornings vanishing.

"As it doesn't have a school, you need to send Colleen to St. Margaret of Scotland, just over in the Shaw neighborhood. You can actually walk there from here. You'll find in nice weather that most people do. I've already contacted the principal on your behalf and the school is holding a spot for Colleen for next August. Brad said that's his parents' parish. I asked him yesterday. They're right off of Flora, aren't they?"

"Yes. But his dad's Jewish."

"But isn't he Catholic? You met him in high school."

One thing about San Diego was that, unlike St. Louis, people hadn't been so fixated on where people went to high school or what Catholic parish you were in, or what temple if you were Jewish. Sure there were protestants in St. Louis, but Catholics dominated the St. Louis landscape as they did in Boston.

"Mom, just because we all went to Bishop DuBourg doesn't mean he's Catholic. I've never asked him. Never seemed relevant. Maybe he is. I don't know."

Her mom shrugged. "Well, these things don't really matter anymore in this day and age. He's still welcome at our fish fry. In fact, your dad and I could use your help with that. And Brad's if he wants. The more the merrier. It's for a good cause."

Her mom ran the roost and Scarlett realized her dad was right. If she didn't set the boundaries quickly, her mom would have Scarlett's life planned out for the next five years.

"Mom . . ." Scarlett caught her dad's amused expression and sighed in exasperation. "I haven't even been home twenty-four hours and you've got playdates and fish fries set up. Can you at least let me unpack and get settled?"

Her mother wasn't in the slightest bit put off. "Don't want the grass to grow under your feet."

"It's February and the grass is dead," Scarlett pointed out drolly.

"Exactly." Her mom missed the gist, whether intentionally or not was anyone's guess. "Our first fish fry is the twentieth."

"Today's only the fourth. I think. Have we even had Fat Tuesday?" Scarlett wasn't really sure. She'd lost track of the days once her entire routine had been to get up, pack, eat, pack, sleep, repeat.

"Not yet. You're in luck that you picked a good month to come. Colleen will love the pet parade. That's next Sunday in Soulard. Then there's the Mardi Gras parade, but that's probably too risqué for her, although the city has worked very hard to make it a family event. So, can we plan on at least attending the pet parade?"

"Sure," Scarlett conceded, before her human-bulldozer mother piled on more things. Colleen would love the pet parade. Scarlett had no objections there.

"Perfect. We'll do mass the night before."

"Mom . . ." Scarlett protested. "Enough. I don't need you giving me something to do each day. I've been on my own since eighteen. Todd's been gone two years. Let me do this. I'm an adult."

"Okay, fine." Her mom shooed an invisible fly. "I'm just so excited you're home. Our visits to California weren't nearly enough and you never came home once because flying cost too much. I've always wanted both of my children near me. We need to make up for lost time."

"Bernadette, they have lives of their own too," her

father inserted, guiding the conversation safely to a close. "Scarlett, we are here to help you with the house. What do you need us to do?"

"Colleen's bedroom. I really want that done today. She slept with me last night, but I want her to feel at home in her new room and start sleeping in there. She's a big girl now."

"Then let's get going," her dad said. "Lead the way."

Chapter Three

By a little after four, Scarlett felt somewhat accomplished. Colleen's room was at 90 percent finished. White bookshelves now brimmed with books, stuffed animals and dolls. Her father had installed white decorative shelves on the walls and hung pictures. Clothes waited on hangers in the closet and found folded neatly inside drawers.

After a forty-minute break for lunch, she and her parents had worked straight through. They'd even hung the curtains that matched Colleen's pink-and-white floral bedspread. Those were mostly decoration, for Colleen's two windows looked at the brick exterior wall of the house next door. She wouldn't even need a shade or mini blinds for privacy. The back bedroom would have had a better view out over the yard, the garage and alley, but this way Colleen was closer. They could always move her things into the back bedroom later, when she was older.

Scarlett caught herself. She had to stop making long-range plans. This arrangement wasn't permanent. Her phone buzzed with a text. *At back door. Can I come in?*

In the chaos she hadn't heard the bell. *Sure,* she texted back to Brad.

He appeared upstairs within seconds. "Hey. Looking good."

He'd meant Colleen's room, but Scarlett flushed anyway.

"Hi, Brad!" Colleen said, diverting his attention. "My room is all pretty!"

"It is." Brad's gaze swept over all the pink and white before returning to Scarlett. "Did you hear the bell?"

Scarlett shook her head. "No."

He frowned. "Okay. Good to know. When I put in the alarm system, I wired it so it could handle an intercom system that was tied to the doorbell. I'll get that installed ASAP. That way you'll know when someone's at the door if you're up here. Need to go sand and mud upstairs. Do you mind?"

"Of course not," her mom said before Scarlett could speak.

But Brad waited for Scarlett's confirmation. "Go ahead," she told him. "We're done here. I'm about to start fixing dinner."

"Which you must stay for," her mother insisted. "And do not say no."

"I'd like that, if you don't mind." Brad again looked to Scarlett for confirmation. He'd been about to protest, Scarlett knew.

"It's fine," she said."

"Great. I'll only be about thirty minutes."

"What are you doing?" her father asked.

"Come up and see," Brad offered. He led the way to the staircase, and everyone followed. Once they reached the landing, the third floor opened up. Ceilings up here were ten feet at their highest point, and like on the first floor, there were three rooms, each with dormer windows. He'd also installed skylights, which were currently covered with snow, making the heavy glass appear dappled gray. Despite this, the third floor was filled with bright light. "These two rooms are finished, as is the bathroom." He opened a primed white six-panel door, still in need of the final coats of paint. While not as large as the bathrooms on the lower floors, this bathroom still had a good-sized sink, shower and toilet. Light came in through a round skylight. "I envisioned this floor as a sort of his-and-her office space, along with a playroom," Brad said. "So I made some built-in bookcases for toy storage."

In the front room, Brad had created built-in shelves using two-by-fours and drywall. They were a seamless part of the wall, and had recessed lighting. He'd also surrounded the window overlooking Victor Street with built-in shelves, and he'd created a huge window seat in the process. Scarlett could already envision the cushion and curling up with Colleen to read her favorite story. "It still needs two more coats," Brad said.

"This is great work," Scarlett's dad said. "Need some help? We can let the ladies make the dinner."

"I can help," Scarlett offered.

"Do you know how to sand?" her father asked.

"No. But I'd like to learn so I can be of use."

"I'll teach you next time," Brad offered, sensing her disappointment.

"Okay. Come on, Colleen," Scarlett said, and they made their way down to the kitchen.

"Who knew he could be so handy," her mom gushed. Brad had already won her mom over. But then he'd easily charmed most women. The fact he'd been somewhat standoffish with Scarlett had always rankled. "I wonder where he learned to do all this. Todd didn't have these skills, did he?"

"No. But Todd came from a family of teachers, remember? They lived in Richmond Heights."

"Have you talked to them since you came back?"

"Not yet. Did I tell you they both retired last June? Sold the house and moved to an apartment in Clayton so they could travel. They'll be back in town a day or two after the twentieth. They left in mid-January for a month in Australia and New Zealand."

"Must be nice," her mom remarked.

"Mom," Scarlett warned. "What else are they supposed to be doing? Todd was their miracle baby and only child and he's gone. I'm glad Larry and Louise went on a dream trip. They deserve it. They can't take their money with them."

"They could put some money in a fund for Colleen."

"Colleen is never going to have to worry about paying

for college. That's all taken care of. It's actually the one thing I don't have to worry about." Scarlett washed the pork chops and set them on a plate. "And she Skypes with them all the time, so she hasn't forgotten them any more than she's forgotten you."

"I wasn't worried about being forgotten." Her mother opened the Viking stove. Peered inside. "Has this ever been used?"

"I highly doubt it," Scarlett replied, opening cabinets and looking for her spices.

"This thing must have cost a fortune. He certainly went for top-of-the-line with these appliances."

Scarlett had no idea. She'd given up looking at those home magazines years ago because all they did was depress her. "Surely it can't be that hard to set the rack in the right place and turn on the broiler."

"Have you looked inside this thing?" her mother asked.

Scarlett set down the spice containers she'd found and came over to peer into the oven. "Wow."

"Exactly." Her mother maneuvered a rack. "This must be how the other half live."

"Well, if he's going to sell the house for top dollar down the road, it has to be done well," Scarlett defended.

"Why would he even want to sell? It's perfect. Besides, the market hasn't recovered this much."

Scarlett studied the control panel. Pressed some buttons. The broiler came to life. Success! She'd won this round. "I've got to get the pork chops seasoned. What else did you bring?"

"I made mashed potatoes last night and we had leftovers, so I brought them. There's some cans of green beans in that pantry over there."

Scarlett took out two cans. Set them on the counter. Went back to readying the pork chops.

"Can I help, Mommy?" Sitting at the island, Colleen had finished coloring a picture.

"After you hang up your picture. I saw a magnet . . ." Scarlett opened a drawer and then another one. Then stopped. The refrigerator was built-in. "Oh honey, this refrigerator doesn't have a front."

Colleen's lips quivered as the enormity of the move hit. She held her picture, which was of a bunch of snowflakes, trees and a three-story house. "Where am I going to put my pictures? I drew our new home."

One thing about four-year-olds, they could easily turn into two-year-olds if stressed enough. "We'll work something out," Scarlett said, trying to avert a meltdown. "What if Granny opens the green beans and you pour them into the pot?"

"But where is my picture going?" Colleen's voice inched higher.

"We will hang it later. We'll get a bulletin board. Put it . . ." She glanced around the kitchen. "We'll hang it over there."

"I want to hang it now," she insisted. "Our new house needs my pictures."

"Come pour green beans." Scarlett's mom tried to

divert her granddaughter.

But Colleen wasn't having any of it. She was tired from a long trip. Her entire life had been uprooted. She could sense her mother's tension and reluctance. It really was the tiny things, like the straw that broke the camel's back, which caused childhood meltdowns. Overwhelmed, Colleen began to cry. "I want to go home."

"Tolerance limit exceeded," Scarlett mumbled, seasoning the pork chops forgotten. She lifted her daughter into her arms. "Shh. I miss San Diego too, but this is our home now."

"I liked our old house." Colleen sniffed. "I didn't get lost."

Me too, Scarlett thought. Although, she'd been adrift since Todd's death. Maybe even before. "You won't get lost here. And you always wanted to live in a castle. And we worked so hard on your new room. It's so pretty."

Her mother had made herself as invisible as she could, all while finishing the pork chops and putting them under the broiler. Now she opened the green beans. The mashed potatoes would microwave. Scarlett, grateful her mom had let her handle this, continued to hold Colleen, although she was getting heavy. "I want my old room," Colleen said, but the tears were lessening somewhat.

Footsteps sounded on the back stairs and the last one squeaked as Brad and her father entered the room. "What seems to be the problem?" her dad asked.

"I want my old room," Colleen repeated.

Brad frowned. "She's just overwhelmed and tired,"

Scarlett inserted hastily. "Please don't think she's ungrateful. Too much change in too short of a time. She lost it when she and I realized there's no place to hang her picture."

Brad's forehead smoothed. He stepped forward. Picked up the picture from the island. "This picture?"

Colleen nodded. "I drew it of my new house."

"We usually hang her art on the refrigerator," Scarlett told him. "We'll have to work out a new place."

"How about for now we put it right here?" Brad found the empty space between a door frame and a window, the same one where Scarlett had indicated a bulletin board could go. He held the picture up. "Would this spot work?"

"Really, you don't need to . . ." Scarlett said, but Brad pulled open a drawer, removed a thumbtack, put the picture in place and jabbed the tack through.

"There. Is that better?" he asked Colleen.

Colleen's green eyes widened and she nodded. The last of her sobs ceased. The round silver thumbtack and a four-year-old's crayon artwork seemed an anomaly in the perfect designer kitchen. Scarlett winced. "There's a hole . . ."

Brad shrugged. "Which spackles and is so tiny anyway. I'll build a small bulletin board for this space. I'll run it from almost the top of the door frame down to about here." He pointed to two feet from the floor. "That way she can reach it too."

"Yay," Colleen said, already happy again.

"What a great idea," Scarlett's mom added. The look she shot Scarlett warned her not to protest.

"See, I never would have thought of that, but it's a perfect addition to this space," Brad continued. "You really helped me, Colleen."

"Yay," she said, simply enthralled by Brad. "That's a picture of our new house."

"It's a beautiful picture. I'm working tomorrow, but I can pick up the materials and build it Friday. Is that okay? Can you wait that long?"

Colleen nodded, her eyes still so wide with awe of Brad. She'd agree to anything; he'd charmed her so thoroughly. Begrudgingly Scarlett had to admit he'd handled her meltdown perfectly. "Good, because after that, I'm a bit busy. I've got this charity stuff I have to do."

"What stuff?" Scarlett asked, curious.

"Stuff for the calendar."

She frowned. She hated feeling stupid. "What calendar?"

His eyebrow arched. "You mean you haven't seen it? Heard about it?"

She felt even more clueless. "I have no clue what you're talking about."

"He's talking about the Sexy Public Servants of St. Louis calendar," her mom said. "It's pretty hot."

"Bernadette." Scarlett heard the resigned sigh in her father's voice, as if he'd been saying her name for years.

"You have to be the only one in the city who hasn't seen or heard about it," Brad added, clearly awed.

Scarlett knew exactly the frustration Colleen had experience earlier. "I have no idea what either of you is talking about. I haven't been here. San Diego, remember?"

"He's Mr. July," her mom called.

Scarlett snapped her head around. Her jaw dropped. "July? You're in the calendar? How could you not have told me once in all the time we were on the phone?"

"Because it's awful. The STLFD picked me and I'm wearing nothing but swim trunks and a smile and standing in front of the river and Eads Bridge. It's embarrassing."

The thought of seeing him in nothing but swim trunks sent her libido into a tailspin. She failed to keep the incredulity out of her voice. "You posed in front of the bridge? For a calendar?"

He exhaled a fast breath. "No. Yes. I was in a studio last June. They Photoshopped the background. Still, I look ridiculous."

"He looks hot," her mother mouthed behind Brad. She fanned her face and Scarlett's dad rolled his eyes.

Scarlett grinned. "Mr. July, huh? I'm going to have to find it. Google will help."

"Don't you dare," he warned.

"Oh, but I must," she teased, because like Colleen, her earlier frustration had been abated. "Makes me wonder what else you haven't told me. Do you moonlight at Chippendales?"

"The simple fact is I didn't have much choice. I'm already way over it, and I've had to attend all these charity-related events ever since. Like the upcoming Mayor's Ball two weekends from now, on Friday the thirteenth. Black tie at the City Hall rotunda. Then there was the calendar ball before that, and the thing at New Year's I managed to get out of because I was working. And thankfully I'm working Valentine's Day, or I'd be stuck on the Mardi Gras float tossing out beads like some of the other guys are." He shuddered and a piece of dark hair swooped down. He brushed it back.

"Sounds terrible," Scarlett chided, still imagining him wearing only swim trunks. "You and your poor celebrity."

Brad frowned. Shoved his hands into his jean pockets. "I never signed up to be a celebrity. The only thing I want to do is my job and now women come up to me and ogle me."

"Women have always come up to you. You were a girl magnet."

"Not like this. They're aggressive. Suggestive. It's like I need a bodyguard to fend them off."

"Todd told me you liked female attention."

"Maybe ten years ago when I was twenty," Brad shot back. "We all grow up sometime."

"Perhaps you should take Scarlett with you next Friday?" her mother suggested, ever the peacekeeper. The dinner plates gave an extra clatter as she took them from a cabinet. "She could fend them all off. It would also give you some time away from the house to discuss things. James and I will babysit. Would you like that, Colleen? If Granny babysat so Mommy could go to a ball?"

Colleen had been watching the exchange the entire time, and Scarlett's stomach dropped. Only back in St. Louis one day and all her good parenting went out the window. "Granny can babysit," Colleen confirmed and she clambered down out of her mom's arms, all better now that the picture was on the wall. "Whatcha doing?" she asked her grandmother.

"I'm about to get the mashed potatoes and microwave them. Want to help?"

"Yes," Colleen said.

"While we work, you two can plan your date."

"It's not a date," Scarlett said. She met Brad's intense gaze and swallowed. Hard.

His full attention was focused on her and the prickle of awareness traveled her spine. "Really, you don't need to do . . ." Brad began.

"I think it's a great idea," her father chimed in, cutting off Brad's protest. "Scarlett needs to get out of the house. You still have your gowns from the military balls. I saw them upstairs. It will do you good to get out on the town. Have some fun."

"I have fun," Scarlett protested.

"When was the last time?" Her mother accompanied that with an arch of an eyebrow. "Listen to your father. Brad, take Scarlett. She could help you out and she needs to be social. It'll give you a chance to reconnect face-to-face. You haven't seen each other in what? Two years?"

Brad could tell when he was trapped. Yet, this wasn't all bad. A good opportunity, in fact. A step in the right direction for honoring Todd's last wishes. "I'd like it if you'd accompany me," he said. "Would you join me at the Mayor's Ball?"

Scarlett also knew when she was beaten. Besides, she owed Brad something for letting her live here. He'd come up with a plan when she'd been looking at having to move back in with her parents. Surely she could help him out with this one thing.

"I'll treat you to a mani-pedi and a haircut," her mother threw out.

"Well, how can I refuse then with those freebies?" She shot Brad a slight smile, and was again disconcerted by the stark intensity she saw in his brown eyes. She found herself once again remembering their brief kiss and suddenly had the urge to scratch beneath the surface and see what made him tick, especially now that there was nothing to stop her. She lived in his house. They had to coexist. They'd reconnected on the phone. But for the tiniest second, she hesitated. Then she threw open Pandora's box and said, "I'd be honored to join you."

His intensity never wavered—it was as if he could see through her, almost as if seeing something she couldn't. "Great," Brad replied. "Then we have a date."

A date. Now that she'd committed, those two words sent both a jolt of panic and a flutter of excitement racing through Scarlett. She'd started dating Todd in October of her freshman year. She'd missed the whole dating scene. Then again, *date* was a word loosely used. Brad needed someone to accompany him, that was all. A buffer to ward off the overzealous women who saw him as a sex object from a picture in a calendar. They'd be out of luck no matter what—Brad wasn't the staying kind. He hadn't had a long-term relationship since he'd left for the Navy. Not that she kept track of his love life. While she'd known Brad since high school and hung out with him and Todd, he'd always been aloof. Distant. During their recent conversations, she still sensed he held something back.

Her mother pulled the pork chops out from the broiler, and the microwave dinged that the potatoes were reheated. The scene held an undercurrent of promise, of simple pleasures brought by spending time with good friends and family. She found the glasses and began to pour everyone water. One great thing about moving home—St. Louis had some of the best-tasting tap water anywhere in the country. Perhaps the future wouldn't be so bad, after all, if she gave it half a chance.

***

As they ate broiled pork chops, microwaved mashed potatoes and canned green beans, Brad couldn't remember a better meal. Zoning regulations meant his apartment kitchen was a sink, mini-fridge, hotplate and a microwave. His bathroom was simply a toilet crammed into a tiny closet beneath the eaves and a shower where he had to duck his head to get under the spray, that was if it was working. In fact, his above-the-garage abode was simply a one-room studio, the only one like it on this block.

She'd agreed to accompany him to the dance. The thought thrilled. They'd attended dances together before, but she'd been with Todd and he'd had a date, usually some redhead or brunette. He never dated blondes. Ever.

There was only one blonde who'd ever attracted his interest and Scarlett had been off-limits. In one part of his mind, she still was off-limits. She'd been Todd's wife. The other part wanted nothing more than to pursue her and make her his.

He had Todd's instructions, one of which read, *You know Scarlett. She'll wallow. Make sure you get her out of the house. Make sure she laughs and has fun.*

He now had the perfect opportunity to do just that.

Her dad said something, and everyone seated around the dining room table laughed. Brad joined in, and then caught Scarlett's gaze. She smiled at him, and it was like a punch to his gut. She was his dream woman. Always had been.

Think of her as a mission, Brad told himself as her green eyes crinkled and laugh lines formed around lips he'd long fantasized about kissing again, this time something more than a stolen moment beneath the high school stairs, swiped before his best friend made his move, a move Brad had known Todd planned to make. Brad had known it was selfish, but he couldn't stop himself. He'd wanted one taste, figuring it would get her out of his system.

It hadn't.

In a mission, feelings had no place. You needed to follow reason. Intuition. In the SEALs, letting morality and emotions factor into an equation could lead to death and often had. SEALs could look back at missions where brethren had died because they'd done something as simple as releasing a child, which in turn had brought down upon them the full force of hell. Brad hadn't been in any of those situations, but Todd had. He knew his best friend had purged his conscience with lots of alcohol.

Yet, when it had come right down to it, despite all of Brad's best persuasive abilities, Todd had reenlisted. Signed back up early with only minor hesitation when considering the wife and child he would be leaving behind for a major part of the year. In hindsight, Brad realized it was almost as if Todd was afraid of married life, afraid of how to be father and husband in the normal, everyday world where bullets flying overhead weren't a common occurrence.

Perhaps Todd hadn't wanted to bring home any baggage, or admit to some of the things he'd done. As it was, he'd been deployed approximately eight months at a time, so by the time he'd gotten somewhat settled into domesticity, it had been time to hit the road and head back overseas.

Maybe some men never outgrew the wanderlust. What was that about the grass being greener on the other side of the proverbial fence? Brad had wanted what Todd had—a wife and kid. A stable, loving home. Someone back in the States that worried and cared—someone besides his mom. Yet despite his best efforts to forget Scarlett, Brad couldn't, and subsequently all other women paled in comparison. Todd had had the commitment that Brad sought, but his friend had run from it, for his mistresses—the sea and his job—captured his interest more than his wife.

The irony rankled.

"Want some help with that?" Brad asked after Scarlett's parents left. He gestured to the dishwasher. A skeptical eyebrow arched as he read her expression. "What? Did Todd never help? I take it dishes weren't his forte. And you don't have to rinse the dishes first. Not with this model or that detergent."

She answered by handing him a plate, which he slid between the bottom rack tines. "Can't save the world in everything," Scarlett quipped, quickly handing him another plate.

"Well, just call me Mr. Domestic. I'm the new kind of superhero. My mother would be proud."

"Well, you saved the day tonight. Thanks for pinning up that picture."

"Anytime. My mother covered our refrigerator. Sometimes whole layers of things fell off because the magnets couldn't hold them. I didn't even think about that when I installed the appliances. See, I told you that your living here would help me out."

He loaded more plates. Put the glasses that came his way on the top rack. Occasionally their fingers would touch, the transfer creating a pleasurable little zing.

"You really didn't have to stay and help," she told him as she passed over a set of forks.

"I'm actually having fun. It's nice to see someone enjoying the kitchen. I'm glad you're here."

Spoons came his way instead of a reply.

"So you're really in agreement with my parents? Now

that we're alone, it's okay. You can back out. You don't have to take me to this ball." She faced him and folded her arms over her chest. "Unless you want to."

"Yes, I really do want to take you. Why not? Have you dressed up in a while? I haven't. I could use a night on the town and it sounds like you could too."

"True. My nights are mainly spent watching kid shows and playing with Colleen. Some adult company might make a nice change."

"Even if it's mine?"

She gave him a shy smile. "You're a gorgeous man. I'll be the envy of every woman there, Mr. July." She snickered at that.

"Ha-ha. Funny." *She'd called him gorgeous.* "You try being exposed to the world."

She made a face. "No, thanks. But I will fend them all off for you. Promise."

"Good. And I promise we'll have fun." Something hovered in the air, something intangible, like hope or promise. She stood far too close—her perky button nose upturned toward his, her tempting lips reachable in one quick swoop. Far too much too soon. He reached forward and brushed a bubble from her cheek. Her mouth parted. "Soap," he said.

"Thanks."

She wouldn't thank him if she knew how much he wanted to kiss her. He checked his desire. "Hey, just so you know, right now I only have a half bath over there as the shower is leaking and I haven't figured out why so I've been using the hall bath upstairs. I was keeping my clothes in the spare bedroom, but I can use the firehouse from here out or my parents'."

Those golden strands framed her face as she shook her head and his fingers itched to touch. Was it as soft and silky as it looked? "No, it's fine. I don't want to put you out any more than I already have. Come get a shower. No need to disrupt your routine. We're your guests."

Even warm reassurance could make him go mad with want. "You aren't guests," he said, for he could never see her that way. "I want you to consider this your home. That's why I'm telling you it'll be around six thirty a.m. when I pop in. You can say no. I won't be put out."

Not by her. For her he'd walk miles, but the flickering in her eyes revealed she wasn't ready to believe him. And why should she? He'd kept her at a distance simply to protect his own sanity. "Okay. I'll probably sleep right through your shower time and if I don't, eventually I'll get used to it and I will. I want us to coexist peacefully."

"I also do laundry here. And my mail will come through the front slot."

"Now you're really pushing it," she said, adding a grin to indicate she was joking. She touched his arm and ran her fingers for a moment over the woven fabric. Then she removed her hand quickly, as if she'd received the same static shock he had. "Seriously, we'll work it out. It's a process. I doubt we'll figure out all the ins and outs of this relationship in one conversation. God knows Todd and I couldn't."

Todd, who would always be a mutual loss. "He loved you very much."

"I know. He was a good man. He cared for you as well. But Todd did what Todd wanted." Silence fell, both lost for a moment to his and her respective thoughts. Her chin jutted forward. "Let's not dwell on the past. Not tonight. I'm sure we'll have plenty of time for that later."

"Okay." He wanted to make her happy. He'd never had that particular urge toward a woman before, unless it was regarding sex. He made sure any woman he chose to bed was well satisfied. But that was as far as it went. However, with Scarlett, all aspects of her happiness came first. He wanted to see her have fun. Smile. Enjoy life again, and not just because he'd made a promise to Todd.

"So how do you make a bulletin board anyway?"

"Framing materials and some cork."

She motioned to the center of the room. "You've done a beautiful job on this place. I can't even imagine what it looked like before."

This was a safe topic, one he embraced. "A huge mess. I went room by room and gutted it down to the studs. And I replaced a lot of those. It's been doable because of the historic tax credits."

"Ah. Well, it's gorgeous."

"Glad you like it."

"I love it."

"Good." Satisfaction filled him. For two years he'd built this house with her in mind. Envisioned her living her and designed everything around her suggestions.

Then his brow creased. When put like that, he worried he was obsessive. More stalker than wooer. He stepped toward the back door, needing space. It was one thing to imagine things from afar, to fantasize and dream. To make believe. It was quite another thing to see those plans coming to fruition, to have the reality come true. She was here, and they had a date. What if said reality failed to meet expectations? What if all these feelings he had towards her were just figments in his mind? A delusion? What then? The large kitchen seemed claustrophobic. "I should go. Dishes are done and it's late. Call or text me if you need anything."

"I don't want to bother you." Her smile wavered as he took another step back. Had he sounded cold? Aloof? He hadn't intended that. Several women had called him an unfeeling bastard, and he knew they were right. He jerked a hand through his hair. He feared he'd hurt Scarlett before they'd even had a chance to really get to know each other, before he had his chance.

"You could never be a bother. Seriously, call me anytime. If I don't answer, it means I'm on a fire call and I'll get back to you right away," he said.

She appeared more reassured. "Okay."

"Promise me."

She smiled then. "Okay. Promise."

He let out a whoosh of pent-up breath. "Perfect. You can depend on me. I'm here for you. I want to be here for you."

"Thanks. That means a lot."

Although deep down Brad knew he wasn't a knight in any type of shining armor. He moved back into her space then and planted a kiss on her forehead. Her skin was soft and smelled of soap. "Sleep well." He drew away, grabbed his coat and made sure not to look back.

Until she called to him when he was halfway out the door. "Oh, Brad." A blast of air swirled in.

"Just so you know, I'm going to find that calendar." She smirked at him, and something inside him bloomed.

"Not if you know what's good for you," he teased back.

"How do you know it wouldn't be?"

And therein lay the trouble. "Good night, Scarlett."

"You too," Scarlett called, clearly pleased she'd won that round of . . . could it have been flirtation? Or just fun between platonic friends?

Brad closed the backdoor behind him, lifted the parka collar to keep out the wind and made his way across the small backyard to the garage. He unlocked his door, went upstairs to the studio apartment which needed a good rehab, and turned on a lamp. Immediately he saw sitting on the table the letters he'd removed from the envelope in his locker.

They would have fun, he determined. Because Todd wanted it that way, and Brad owed it to Todd. He also owed it to himself. Finally, once and for all, he needed to either see if his love for her was real, or if it was just something he'd built up in his head. He prayed for the former and feared the latter. Time would tell.

Chapter Four

Scarlett bought a new dress. Not that there was anything wrong with her two other gowns. But when she'd taken them out of the storage box and lifted the clear, protective dry-cleaning plastic, her eyes had begun to water. She'd sniffled. Then she'd simply let herself have a short cry, until Colleen had come into the third bedroom and asked, "What's wrong?"

Scarlett had wiped away the tears and lied that she'd gotten dust in her eye. Then she'd pulled out the dresses and told Colleen about each of the events she'd attended with Todd. She told her about the delicious food. The dancing. How handsome her daddy had looked in his fancy dress uniform. She'd even let Colleen step into her glittery sequined heels and trot around, laughing as her daughter clacked on the hardwood floors, her pink painted toes peeking through the hole. Her daughter's antics always cheered her up, and soon Scarlett stowed the dresses safely back in their plastic wrapping, hung them in the closet and closed the door. She'd donate them at some point, but not yet.

She spun around and gave herself one last look in the mirror. Her mom had taken her out for a day of pampering. She'd been scrubbed, buffed and professionally made up. Her wavy hair was up in a knot, although two wispy tendrils draped by each ear. Smokey eyelids blinked. Red lips pouted, the color somehow not too orange—the makeup artist had been correct when she'd insisted Scarlett try the bold shade. As she stared at her reflection, she had no idea who this pretty woman was. Hadn't ever seen her before.

"You look like Cinderella." Colleen sat on the closed toilet lid, her own lips stained pink with a swipe of Scarlett's usual shade. "But she wore glass slippers."

"I feel like Cinderella," Scarlett admitted. She touched her bare throat. The midnight blue dress had a higher, more modest neckline, and she'd decided against a necklace. Pearls would be out of place, and except for a thin gold chain, she really didn't have anything that wouldn't appear shabby. No, better to go without. Besides, she did have earrings, and she touched the small diamond studs, her only real piece of jewelry and a gift from Todd after he'd received the SEAL bonus.

"You're beautiful, Mommy."

"You think so?" She held out her hand and Colleen took it. Skirt swishing mid-calf, she led her daughter out to their second-floor living room.

"Brad will think you're beautiful too."

That assertion made Scarlett's heart jump, which was silly. Despite living in his house, she'd hardly seen him this week. If he had come in to shower before work—and she knew he had because the alarm on the intercom system he'd installed had beeped—he moved like a ghost. He'd drywalled the third floor. A bulletin board had appeared, with Colleen's picture tacked up dead center. Now the board he'd built was full of crayon artwork. The beeping of the alarm being armed had told her when he'd left. The few times they'd passed, he'd smiled at her and then looked away. It was like he was avoiding her, sort of like he'd done in high school after she'd started dating Todd.

The intercom buzzed, indicating someone had pushed the back doorbell. "He's here."

"Or maybe it's Granny again," Colleen said, following her mom down to the kitchen door.

Or maybe both, Scarlett thought as she saw Brad and her mother standing on the back porch. "Look who I found," her mom said as she entered first. "He was right behind me on the walk."

"Brad!" Colleen shouted. "You're all dressed up."

Scarlett swallowed as butterflies began to thump against her chest. He wore a black tux that fit like a glove, completed with a black tie and cummerbund. He'd added some gel or something, his hair combed back from his face and tucked behind his ears. Had he gotten a trim? She tamped down the desire to thread her hands into that hair, for Brad was a friend. Friend with a capital *F.*

Although flirting also began with an *F,* which they had been doing the other night. Or so she thought. She'd replayed their good-bye in the kitchen over and over before chalking it up to renewing old acquaintances.

"Had to dress up," he told Colleen, reaching over to ruffle her hair. "It's a black tie event. Had to wear this monkey suit."

"You don't look like a monkey. Monkeys have bigger ears and lots of fur."

"It's just an expression," Scarlett tried to explain. "Means he feels silly."

Colleen processed this. Brightened. "Oh. Mommy, do you feel like a monkey? You're all dressed up too."

"No," she said.

"Your mommy is too pretty to be a monkey." Brad's eyes darkened as his gaze roved over Scarlett, and unable to help herself, she blushed. "I don't remember seeing that dress in any of the pictures."

"It's new."

"New city, new life, new dress," her mother added. "Speaking of pictures, stand over there and let me take one." Bernadette took out her phone and gestured them together. Brad wrapped his arm around Scarlett's waist. Such an innocent gesture, but Scarlett felt her face flame as he drew her to him. Her knees weakened and she wrapped her arm around him. He was a few inches taller than Todd, but with her heels she fit against him fine. As if she belonged there.

"Smile," her mom directed. "One . . . two . . . three . . ."

She leaned back and checked the phone screen. "Perfect." She made a shooing motion. "Now both of you get out of here and go have a good time. You're cutting into my grandma time."

"Yes, ma'am." Brad extended his arm to indicate Scarlett should go first. Flustered from the effect of one brief touch, she stepped forward and grabbed her long, black wool coat. "Here, let me," he offered.

He held it open and she stepped in, his fingers lightly grazing the nape of her neck as he settled the coat on her back. A delightful shiver ran down her spine. "Thank you," she said, taking another step forward. Fingers fumbled with the buttons. One tiny tickle of him touching her skin and her whole body had gone haywire.

She stepped out in the brisk night air, the weather on this Friday the thirteenth having turned colder. "So much for it being decent for the Mardi Gras parade tomorrow. We got lucky with the pet parade last weekend. That was in the mid-fifties."

"Yeah," Brad said. "Felt like a heat wave once the snow melted. But later tonight the wind's going to shift. It's going to get even colder. Maybe even have some more snow later in the week."

"Lovely," Scarlett said. "I hate snow. Why did I move here again?"

"So you could go to this fancy schmancy ball with me and save me from all the hordes of crazy women wanting my body."

"Oh yes," Scarlett teased back, trying not to think of

his body. "I'd almost forgotten."

"Her indifference wounds me," Brad joked. He placed a guiding hand on her back and they walked to his Honda Pilot, which he'd backed out of the garage. Scarlett's mom was parked next to the Prius on the extra parking pad. He opened the passenger door, reached in, and removed a square, white box from the front seat. "I thought you might like one of these."

"Thank you." Touched, Scarlett opened the box, and thanks to the streetlights, could see that he'd bought her a Mardi Gras–themed wrist corsage made of purple-and-gold ribbon and orange roses. "It's beautiful. I'll put it on when we get there." Brad assisted her into the car and shut the door behind her. "So no uniform?" she asked, meaning his firefighter dress attire. Todd had always been in his dress uniform for military balls.

"Not for this." Brad put on his seat belt and she did the same.

"Well, the tux suits you. I may have some difficulty fending them all off."

"Ha."

"I'm serious. You're attractive."

He started the car. "You find me attractive?"

"Well, yes. I'm a woman. Any woman would. You're not ugly."

He backed into the alley. "Gee, that's an endorsement."

"You know what I mean. You're handsome. You look great in that tux. Getting married didn't make me blind. If

I hadn't been with Todd, I would have made a beeline toward you."

"And now?" He eased the SUV out of the narrow alley and onto northbound Grand.

"Well, now I'm the luckiest woman there. I get to be with Mr. July, and it's made even better because he's a good friend. And, no, I still haven't seen the calendar because I unpacked all week and you asked me not to."

"Thanks."

"You're welcome." She'd done it because she wanted them to be friends, and being friends meant showing respect. Scarlett averted her gaze and stared out the passenger window to take in the city she hadn't seen in years while Brad concentrated on traffic out the front. Luckily the Blues hockey team was out of town, so they wouldn't have to compete with hockey fans for spots in the City Hall parking lot. However, Scarlett saw that didn't matter as the event provided a valet service. "Part of the ticket," Brad told her after she asked.

City Hall had opened in 1904, and the front of the Renaissance-revival-style building was all lit up. Purple, green and orange lights cast a festive glow on the massive building. Scarlett had been here only once before—to get a marriage license. After dark, the place transformed like one of those *Night at the Museum* movies, just without the animals and talking statues. The harsh fluorescent lighting was gone—those same colorful lights from outside infused through open space and created patterns on the marble floor. Festive banners draped down pillars. Masks hung suspended in the air. Waiters worked behind strategically placed bars.

People lingered on all floors, with the VIP tables on the second and third floors. Some revelers wore colorful masks complete with feathers and sequins that clearly they'd bought themselves, while others didn't wear even the free masks being handed out. Dresses varied from short to long, with the majority like hers, Scarlett saw with great relief. In fact, it seemed as if almost anything festive was appropriate; some partygoers were even dressed in festive Mardi Gras costumes. As for the men, most were in formal tuxes, although some had opted for brightly colored bow ties in keeping with the Mardi Gras theme. Others wore vests that might be found on a court jester, and many, like Brad, simply wore black tie.

Although, none wore it as well as he did, Scarlett thought as they checked their overcoats. "Wait a minute." Brad drew her to a quiet corner and took the corsage out of the box and placed it on her left wrist. His fingers caressed her wrist and fire spread. "Like it?"

Her mouth had dried, but she got the words out. "I do. Thank you." The hand that held the empty box trembled, and Brad took it from her. He offered her his arm. "Shall we?"

"Yes." They strode across the rotunda floor. He might not be a politician or one of St. Louis's rich elite, but men nodded in greeting. Women smiled appreciatively and gave him long sideways glances. Probably thinking of his exposed torso in the calendar, Scarlett thought. Not that she blamed them. Already, at times, glimmers of interest flickered in her brain—until she uncomfortably shoved them aside. First, it seemed almost like a betrayal of Todd, although she knew that being a widow didn't mean she was dead too. Yet, she didn't grieve like she had in the beginning. The hurt had faded—and for that she felt guilty. Todd had never made her quiver the way a few innocent touches from Brad had. The sizzle from his every contact burned its way through her and she resisted the urge to rub her wrist where it still tingled from his placing the corsage.

"What do you want to drink?" Brad asked as they queued up at the bar. Nearby a juggler entertained a small crowd. Down the way, a mime pretended he was stuck in a box.

She paused. How long had it been since she'd been out? At least two years. Maybe three. That was probably the last time she'd had alcohol, too. Single moms were more likely to curl up with the kids and drink chocolate milk. "I'll take some white wine."

He took her hand and studied the corsage, sending the butterflies in her stomach into flight. "Who knew those colors would work so well? I'll be right back."

Brad headed for the bar and Scarlett worked to calm her nerves. A woman dressed as a harlequin came by and draped a multicolored boa over Scarlett's shoulders. She toyed with the feathers, trying to make sense of how Brad made her body react. She wasn't a giggly young girl. But as he returned, her heart jumped. He turned to hand her a short, plastic wineglass. In his hand, he held a red aluminum Budweiser bottle. He used it to point to the boa. "Where'd you get that?"

She shrugged. The woman was long gone, off to spread the Mardi Gras cheer. "We're up on the third floor. The calendar committee actually reserved some tables for us," Brad told her.

"I guess the view's better."

He grinned. "Well, the high rollers pay more to be on the second floor. The rest of the tables are general admission, first come, first served, I guess. I could simply be feeding you misinformation. This is my first time at this."

"Then our first date is an adventure for both of us." They walked up the wide staircase, and Scarlett was glad he couldn't see her face. Calling something a first date implied there would be a second.

As they ascended, they left the first-floor entertainment behind. "There's supposed to be an acrobatic show before the band begins playing. Heard it's eighties music tonight."

"It all sounds interesting," Scarlett said, taking in everything as she passed by. They found their table, where they were seated with several other calendar guys and their dates or significant others. Scarlett met so many people, she felt like her head spun. There was Taylor Krebs, the calendar photographer, who was engaged to firefighter Joe Marino. They'd met the day of the shoot, when she'd done Brad's photos as well. Scarlett also met veterinarian Kat

Saunders, who was dating animal task force cop Jack Donovan. She and Jack had met at one of the first calendar balls and also bonded over an injured puppy. "We'll probably see you at a lot of these," Kat said. "Being that you're new in town, if you need anything, call me."

"I will," Scarlett promised, the wine and good company allowing her to relax.

The circus show came complete with aerial acrobatics, and the live band followed. She'd been born in the eighties but still recognized many of the songs, although she wasn't singing along like many of the older guests were.

Still, musical era be darned, she hadn't danced in forever, either, and as the heavy bass beat pumped through her, she wanted to dance. So she grabbed Brad's hand. "Let's go dance!"

"Okay." They made their way down to the dance floor and joined the crowd waving their hands. The pounding energy was infectious, and she and Brad stayed out for a second, then a third number.

"This is so great!" Scarlett shouted over the music.

"I know! Glad you're having fun."

"Oh, I am." As a slower song began, Scarlett shook her head. "Let's skip this one. I'm thirsty."

They made their way to the edges, headed back to the bar. "Wine again?"

"Could I have some water too?"

"Sure." Brad took a step and turned back when a voice called her name.

"Scarlett?"

She also turned, hearing her name. "Scarlett O'Reilly. It is you."

"It's Harrison now," she corrected, smiling brightly as the man approached. Tried to place him. Beside her, Brad froze. The man held out his hand in greeting. "It's me. Tommy Rourke. I was, well, still am, a friend of Sean's."

"That's right! Tommy!" Her smile widened and she shook his hand. Her brother's friend had gained about twenty pounds and his hair had started to recede.

"I'm sorry for your loss. Sean told her. "My Karen died three years ago. Leukemia. Been a single dad since then. My Kyle is three."

"My daughter is four. And I remember Karen.:" His wife had been a perky, bubbly basketball star, the type that you couldn't hate or envy because she was simply so darn nice. "She was a senior, I think, when I was a freshman."

Tommy smiled, pleased she'd remembered. "That's right, you also went to DuBourg. Sean and I were at SLUH. Karen and I met at one of those mixers. High school sweethearts. Like you and Todd. And this is . . ."

Scarlett's hand flew in front of her mouth, embarrassed. What must Brad think? Beside her, he stood statue still. "Oh, sorry. Tommy, this is Brad Silverman. He and my husband were best friends. He's technically my landlord. I'm renting his house on Victor. Just off Grand. I moved back a few weeks ago."

"Really? That's not too far from me. Just a few blocks south, if that. St. Pius, right?"

"Yes." Living in San Diego for the past ten years, she'd

forgotten just how much St. Louisans mentioned where they went to high school or where they went to church. It instantly defined your social class.

Tommy sized up Brad, who stood at least eight inches taller. He reached his hand out and Brad shook it. Must have gripped hard because Tommy hid a wince. "Nice to meet you, Brad. Glad you could help Scarlett out." Tommy turned back to Scarlett before Brad could answer. "I don't want to keep you, but I'd love to catch up sometime. Will you be at the fish fry next Friday?"

Scarlett laughed. "My parents are already recruiting me to work the dessert table."

Tommy's smile widened. "Perfect. I'll be there. Never miss it if I can help it. We can catch up then. If I don't see you later, have fun tonight."

"Thanks. You too." Scarlett stared after him as Tommy merged into the crowd. She turned to Brad. "That's a friend of my brother's."

"So I gathered," Brad said, his expression inscrutable.

She frowned. "What?"

"Nothing." Brad shrugged. He'd discarded the suit coat, leaving it at their table while they'd been dancing. He snagged two bottles of water from a roaming waiter.

Scarlett planted her hand on her hip, used the other to hold the bottle of water Brad had gotten. "That's just Tommy. Friend of my brother's."

"You already said that." Brad uncapped his water. She continued to stare at him. He cupped her elbow, moved her out of traffic. "He was hitting on you, that's all."

She frowned. "No, he wasn't. He was being friendly."

"If I wasn't here, he'd be all over you. He's a widower with a kid your daughter's age."

"Which means nothing," Scarlett scolded.

As if choosing his words, Brad took a sip. "It means he's lonely and looking. I know the type."

She really couldn't believe it. Then again, having dated Todd for all of high school and marrying him right after, she didn't have much experience with the opposite sex. "Please. It's nothing to hang out with someone at the fish fry. I'll be serving cake with my mom. Hardly a place where I'm going to be ravaged, wouldn't you agree?"

"It's just ironic that I brought you to fend off the women and it's you who is getting hit on. He asked you out and you don't see it."

"Well, I haven't dated anyone except Todd. I don't know what I'm looking for. I feel as if you're making this my fault."

***

Brad held up the bottle in self-defense. This conversation was not going well. "No. That's not my intention at all. I have no control over you and I know that. I just . . ."

He stopped before he said too much. Todd's instructions were that she be happy. That she find someone so she didn't go through the rest of her life alone. But the moment Brad had walked into her house tonight and seen her standing there, looking like a goddess in her dark blue dress, he'd wanted nothing more than to touch her. He wanted to run his fingers from the dip behind her ear to the indentation at the base of her throat. Then he wanted to replace his fingers with his lips so he could plant kisses on her lovely, creamy skin. He wanted to take the pins out of hair the color of gold and let the waves pool around her shoulders.

She placed her empty water bottle on a nearby table. "Can we dance more? I haven't danced in forever and I'm really enjoying it. I don't want my seeing Tommy to spoil anything between us."

"Sure." Brad added his empty bottle to the collection on the table. Dancing was safe, and he was probably being unreasonable. But the rush of jealousy that had hit him when Tommy had approached had been almost overpowering. For a man who prided himself on his control under pressure, he hated that he'd lost it, even if for a moment.

"I like this song. Let's forget everything and just have fun," she urged.

"Agreed." Brad forced himself to relax. He didn't want to ruin their night. Besides, wasn't that the point of Mardi Gras, to party with abandon until after Fat Tuesday? For once Ash Wednesday and Lent arrived, forty days of piety followed and you were supposed to give something up so you could focus on what the coming of the Lord meant.

Although after leaving Catholic high school, Brad had never been very successful with anything but the debauchery. One time he and some of his SEAL buddies had taken their leave in New Orleans. The endless party had been a good time, what little he remembered of it. Of course, he'd given up his wayward ways pretty quickly. The job had always come first, and he'd tired quickly of that "being out of control" thing. He followed Scarlett onto the dance floor where they joined the crowd belting out the lyrics to Joan Jett's classic "I Love Rock 'n' Roll."

After several songs, the music slowed down. He made a move toward the bar, but a hand on his arm stopped him. She said, placing her hand on his arm, "I like this song."

For a second, Brad stilled. He'd avoided slow dancing with her at her wedding. Put on the spot, he couldn't refuse her without being a schmuck. "You sure you aren't tired?"

She gave him an odd look. "No. You promised me fun. Dance with me. You're not afraid of me, are you?"

"No." *Yes.*

"So what's the problem? Is it still Tommy?"

"No." *It's intimate, that's all.* But he couldn't use that excuse, and he wanted to hold her. And she'd asked him. He led her to the dance floor and gathered her into arms. Slid his hands onto her hips and felt the weight of her arms as she placed them around his neck. He'd held her closer during a brief hug after the funeral, but that had been different. Sobering. Comforting. Almost rote. Expected. Medicinal.

Desire flared through him, sending heat to his groin. His erection pressed into her; he couldn't hide it. Her eyes widened, and she hid her reaction by resting her head on his chest, just below his chin. His hands splayed across the small of her back. The scent of her shampoo filled his nostrils with the aroma of faint vanilla. The skin on the inside of her wrist hinted of apples, roses and musk, a heady combination. They moved in sync to the beat—a step-and-sway motion that seemed as natural as breathing. He wanted her. There was no denying that.

Her green eyes reflected the colorful lights giving the dance floor its club-like atmosphere. She lifted a hand and ran it along his cheek. "Thank you," she said.

Her words caught him by surprise, and he captured her hand, brought it into the narrow gap between them. "For what?"

"Tonight. This." She freed her hand. Gestured to the crowd. Returned to place it against his chest. "Getting out of the house makes me feel alive. Maybe even like someone new. It's all because of you."

"Don't give me any credit. I didn't do anything."

She put the flower corsage under his nose. "You made my night on the town, well, you know. I'm enjoying myself. With you."

Did his heart skip a beat? He knew he almost missed a step. "I'm glad you're here."

"Me too, although you would have been fine going stag."

"Yes, but you being here made it better." He lost himself in her vanilla and jasmine scent. "I want to be your friend, Scarlett. I'd like us to become closer."

She nodded, taking his words at face value. "I'd like

that too."

"I don't want to crowd you." He tightened his grip, pulling her closer against his chest so that he could memorize the feel of her in his arms, relive this moment when the nights were dark and unbearable and sleep didn't exist. She pressed her cheek into his shirt.

Finally she lifted her head again and said, "I don't need space. I need friends. I thought I had them in San Diego. It's one reason I stayed, fought to keep my life there as long as I did. But things change. People treat you differently. They look at you with sympathy in their eyes. Their husbands are still deployed. Yours isn't, and it reminds them of their own vulnerability, that they might be next to have the uniforms at the door. You quickly get the sense that while they like you, it's become awkward whenever you're around."

"I'm sorry," Brad said, meaning it. His fingertips gently kneaded her lower back, as if the small massage could take away her bad memories. "I wish you'd told me when we talked."

"I didn't tell anyone. I didn't want my family to know. I told them I'd be fine, and I wasn't. They were right. I probably should have come home when they insisted."

"Then the house wouldn't have been ready."

"True. Thanks to you I didn't have to move home." A chill shook her.

"Hey, it's okay." He wrapped his arms tighter.

"I know. I love my mom but I didn't want to live with her. That seemed like too much failure."

"You're not a failure."

"I know. But moving in with my parents at my age? That's too much."

"Then things worked out for the best."

"Perhaps they're starting to." Someone bumped her from behind and she tripped forward. Brad caught her. "Hey, I've got you."

"Thanks. You're a good guy, Brad Silverman." She touched his cheek again, in a move that shattered all control. "I hope you know how special you are."

"I'm far from it," he ground out as he hardened again. He ground her to him, letting her see the effect she'd had on him. Her eyes widened. Darkened. "Don't set me on a pedestal," he warned. "I've done things that would curl your toes."

"You're ex-military. Of course you have."

"I've not always been an honorable man."

"But you are now, and that's what matters."

Hell no, he wasn't honorable. Brad wanted to kiss her until her strawberry-colored lips were swollen. As close as she was, her breasts were against his chest, and he wanted to free them from the dress, take them into his mouth and suck on each pretty pebble until it turned into a hard little nub. He wanted to taste her everywhere, to make her cry out in pleasure. Part of him throbbed.

"It fades, you know," she said out of the blue.

"What?" He blinked. Focused.

"The past. The pain."

Oh. She hadn't been meaning that part of him that

was stiff as a board. He mentally gave himself a cold shower as the band began to wrap up the song.

"After it first happened, I didn't even want to get out of bed, which is ridiculous because he wasn't even home for eight months out of the year. But I had to be strong for Colleen. And we had a routine. So I settled back into it, except that there weren't any more Skype sessions. The phone stopped ringing, and only bills were in the mail. It becomes a new normal and you go on."

"I don't know if you ever truly fill the hole." It was a rare admission, one that slipped out only because he'd lost himself in her arms. He tried to shove away the sudden guilt He was here, holding Scarlett and wanting to kiss her, while it should have been Todd.

"You have to figure out how to let go." Scarlett seemed to sense Brad's feelings. But she couldn't know the depths of his despair. "But I will admit it takes a long time. Part of me reached that when I spread his ashes. Yet I'm in a new dress because I couldn't bear to wear one I'd worn with him."

The slow song ended and she stepped out of his arms as the band picked up the tempo. "Another?" he questioned. For she made him want to tell her all about his guilt, tell her his transgressions. And he could never do that.

She patted a wayward strand of hair that had escaped the updo when she'd had her head on his chest. "If you don't mind, I'm actually getting tired. I'm usually in bed shortly after Colleen and I put her to bed at eight thirty."

"Then we can go. I'm up early myself. It is getting late."

"You don't mind?"

"Absolutely not." He voiced the lie, for while it was best, he also wanted to spend as much time as possible with her. But he'd promised her fun and he refused to end on a down note. "So Colleen gets up early?"

"At the crack of dawn. Always has. I adjusted my sleep schedule around hers."

He took his phone out. Glanced at the time. "Well, it's eleven."

"Close enough to midnight that this Cinderella should go home. And you have to work tomorrow."

"I'll be fine. I once went forty-eight hours without any shut-eye."

She appeared horrified. "That's terrible."

"One of the reasons I left the SEALs. Now I usually get about six hours unless I'm on shift. But even then I do get more shuteye than you'd think."

They made their way up to the third floor of city hall, where Brad retrieved his tuxedo jacket from the seat back. A few of their earlier tablemates were still there, so they said their good-byes and headed down toward the coat check, where Brad stood in line with a few others. He hated to see the night end, but he could see the tiredness hidden behind her pretty eyes.

"I really had fun tonight," she told him as the valet brought his Honda around. "Thanks."

"You've already said that."

"I want you to know I really meant it. It bears repeating."

A strange tightness claimed his chest. "Okay. Well, you're welcome. I had fun too. We'll have to do something like this again."

He wanted to make her happy. Always had, and always would, the instructions from Todd truly irrelevant. Pleasing her was as essential as breathing. Much more than any misplaced guilt.

"I'd like that."

"Me too."

She placed a hand on his arm before stepping into the SUV. Turned to him. "I was serious about what I said earlier. I want us to be friends. You were Todd's best friend, and while we hung out, I realized the other day I don't really know you like I'd like. It seems like you deliberately held yourself back."

He had. It had been a defense mechanism to protect a heart lost to her—a love he couldn't reveal as she'd loved someone else. "Sorry," he mumbled. "I didn't want to ever seem inappropriate."

"How would talking to me have been inappropriate?"

"Well, some guys don't like it," he hedged.

"Todd was never the jealous type. And now it doesn't matter. We're going to be sharing a house, well, sort of, so I should know you better. For instance, what's your favorite song?"

"What does that have to do with anything? It's cold. Get inside." The wind blew and he ushered her into the vehicle and closed the door. Stupid St. Louis weather. Tomorrow's parade weather was going to be cold and miserable, as were any outdoor calls he'd have to go on. Yet he knew Mother Nature's nastiness wouldn't stop the parade goers any more than it would stop him from doing his job. He tipped the valet and climbed in.

"You didn't answer my question," she said as he put the car in drive.

"I'm not sure how my favorite song is relevant."

"Do you realize I know nothing about you? I want to get to know you. Peel back a few of your layers. Get to know the guy behind the tool belt."

"Uh, that sounds rather personal."

She laughed. "That came out all wrong. But who cares? I've had wine, I've danced and I'm free, at least for a few more minutes, until I go back to mom time. So play along."

"I'm not that interesting."

"That's not playing along," Scarlett scolded. "Let's do one of those first-thing-that-comes-into-your-head things. I'll answer too. Deal?"

"Will this make you happy?"

She nodded. "Yes."

"Fine."

"Good." She leaned against her seat with a satisfied thump. "We'll start with an easier one then. Like, how do you take your coffee?"

"With cream and sugar. I add it every time I use the coffeemaker." His fingers tightened on the steering wheel.

He could feel Scarlett staring at his profile.

"Now that you mention it, I have noticed that. I add sugar, too, but prefer hot chocolate. Okay, next. Favorite book?"

Living off Grand, they were already halfway home. "I like biographies." He risked glancing at her. Saw her wrinkle her nose, for they were driving under the streetlight. "Clearly you don't like that answer."

"No, it's rare I read about people's lives. Find it boring. Although I did read that Cary Elwes book about making the movie *The Princess Bride*. What's your favorite title?"

"David McCullough's *John Adams*. I read it after it became that HBO miniseries."

The nose wrinkled again, like an adorable rabbit. Instead of being irritated, he had the urge to rub it smooth. "Nope. Never heard of it. So next question. Thing that drives you the most crazy?"

Aside from his desire for her? "Conformity," he said.

"Which is really ironic considering you are in a job that requires all those rules and regulations."

She had him there. "True. We even carry our standard operating procedures manual on the truck. But that doesn't mean I blindly accept things. And I read things and study issues before I go out and vote."

"I like that you have convictions. Says you have character."

He made a left onto Grand. Less than five minutes. He wasn't sure how he felt about that. On one hand, he'd be free from the tight confines of the car. On the flip side, he was enjoying the night and didn't want it to end.

"Favorite holiday?"

"You clearly don't give up."

"Nope." She grinned. "If you don't play nice they're only going to get harder from here."

"Fine. I like Christmas. And I can't stand Valentine's Day."

"Which is tomorrow. So you won't want the card I bought you?"

"You bought me a card?"

"No, but I'm definitely not going to now. I'll make sure Colleen doesn't make you one either. Although, she's pretty good with the crayons."

"You're a minx. Cards would be okay."

"Then you're not as hating of the day as you think."

She had him there. "So you think you know me?"

"Well, isn't that what this is all about?"

He sighed. She'd gotten him again. "Fine, you win. Ask away."

"I will, but first I get to answer. Really, with Colleen, any holiday is special. Last year we made homemade cards for her preschool class. She was so excited, so when you see it through a child's eyes, Valentine's Day becomes far less commercial and a lot more personal."

"Well, we guys are set up to fail. We always worry. Did we get the right gift? Did we pick the right restaurant? All that. And it's hard to send things from the front line." His hands spun the wheel, making the left onto Shenandoah.

"So that song?" she asked.

"George Jones. 'Walk Through This World With Me.' It's a real oldie, but we sang it around the fire during that summer my parents sent me away to camp. I think it was after eighth grade. I thought I was far too cool to be there, but it was pretty fun once I got used to it. My counselor was an aspiring country music star. We'd sing John Denver's 'Take Me Home, Country Roads' too. Ironic that now they sing it in the third period of the Blues games now. Anyway, it was co-ed camp, and I got my first kiss that summer. I wanted her to walk the world with me."

She smiled. "That's so sweet. So romantic."

"Yeah, and right now I feel like I need to go sand some drywall to get some of my manly street cred back."

She laughed. "Aww."

"Yeah, that's right, it was the summer before I met you and Todd. My last time at camp. So you saw me that August. I was a scrawny late bloomer."

"Far from it," Scarlett protested. "I remember thinking wow, he's cute. And then you kissed me." She paused. "I've always wondered why you did that."

"Because I couldn't resist."

She digested that for a moment. "Then why didn't you ask me out?"

"Because Todd was going to. He'd called dibs."

Her voice inched upward. "He called dibs? You negotiated?"

Oh shit. He tried to make light. "Hey, it was years ago, you two were happy, and it's just what guys do." The automatic garage door opened, and he drove inside and parked next to a table saw. "The guy code is important and I followed it."

"But you kissed me."

"Yeah."

"And you knew before you kissed me Todd was going to ask me out."

What was that saying? In for a penny, in for a pound? "Yeah. I did. And frankly, I liked it too damn much, but Todd was all excited about asking you out. And we were in high school. Freshman year. I didn't think you and he would last. If I had, I might have fought harder."

He swung out of the car and opened her door. Took her hand in his and helped her down. She seemed a little shell-shocked. "Any more questions? Oh, I remember. You asked about my favorite band. The Beatles. Isn't that everyone's favorite band?"

Still a bit shell shocked by what he'd told her, she attempted a rally. "Not mine. I prefer the Rolling Stones to the Beatles. And I like U2 best of all. So would you have asked me out if Todd hadn't?"

"Does it matter almost fifteen years later?"

Her hands went onto her hips. Her chin came up. "Yes."

"Maybe."

"Maybe?" She seemed incredulous.

"I said I would have fought harder. It was a good kiss."

"I thought so too."

"You did?" His turn to be surprised.

"Yeah. Made me wonder." She stepped forward, into

his space. He leaned back against the closed car door. "Still makes me wonder. Only one way to find out." She rose onto her tiptoes, snaked her arms around his neck and brought her lips to his.

***

The moment her lips touched his, Scarlett had one thought. The man could kiss. What had happened in high school seemed cartoonish compared to the mouth skill Brad exhibited now. She heard herself moan as he nipped and tugged. Moaned again as he raked his teeth across her tongue, sucking it up inside his mouth. He'd moved his hands to her ass, and he'd pulled her to him—the erection she'd felt while slow dancing again pressed into her belly. He swirled his tongue over her lips, robbing her senses. Her breasts throbbed and heat pooled as she shook as the pleasure consumed. He kneaded her bottom through the coat and she wanted to throw it to the floor so there were fewer layers. Wanted to strip so she could feel him between her legs, let him quench the fire he'd stoked there. He slid his lips down her neck, then came back to capture her mouth again, creating even more heat. His hand moved beneath her coat front and he cupped her breast. Ran a thumb over the nipple that strained to be free, desired to be sucked.

Then her phone began to ring, shattering the moment. She drew back and fumbled in the small clutch, her fingers trembling from the aftereffects of what she'd been doing.

She saw the number, got the call answered before the last ring. "Hello?"

"Scarlett? Are you home? I thought I saw a light out in the garage."

"We just got here. We'll be inside in a minute." She ended the call. Put the phone back in her clutch. Made an inane statement. "I guess the clock chimed twelve."

"What?"

She shook her head. "Nothing. My mom's waiting." Mustering as much dignity as she could manage, she headed to the side door and opened it. Brad followed. "Let me walk you to the door."

"You don't . . ."

"I'll walk you to the door," he insisted.

She led the way up the steps to the back porch. Opened the door, turned off the alarm. Heard footsteps on the stairs. Her mom looked her over. "You appear a bit flushed," she said.

"Brad and I were having a heated conversation," Scarlett lied. "Beatles or Rolling Stones?"

"Beatles," her mom replied with a frown. "Why?"

"You sided with Brad," Scarlett said. "See why our debate was intense?"

Her mom made an apologetic tsk. "Sorry, dear. I still love Paul McCartney to this day. He's a national treasure for England and us."

Scarlett changed the subject. "How was Colleen?"

"Perfect. An angel as always. She's asleep in her own bed. She wanted you to know what a big girl she was."

"Thanks."

Her mom bundled up into her heavy parka. "It's cold out there, I'm sure. I'll talk to you around noon. Planning to sleep in. Sadly no parade for us this year. Last week's pet parade will have to have been enough. At least that was warm."

"I'll walk you out," Brad offered.

"Fine." Her mom glanced around. "Oh. I forgot my purse. Let me run up and get it. I'll only be a minute."

"So we were debating? I've never heard it called that," Brad said.

Scarlett touched her messed-up hair. "Well, it was all I could think of."

A moment of silence fell.

"So are we going to talk about this or ignore it like high school?" Brad asked.

She had no idea how she felt. "Let's table it for another time. I'll say it was again a great kiss and we'll leave it at that, for now. My mom's on her way."

"Okay. Fair. I hope this didn't ruin the night."

He appeared seriously worried, winning him bonus points. The fact he cared what she thought impressed her. "No. Not at all. And I loved dressing up. It's back to sweats by morning."

"You look great in anything. You could wear a sackcloth and I'd…"

She blushed. "Thank you."

He lowered his head, this time giving her a proper good night kiss, which was a light kiss on the lips. Still, an electric shock reverberated through her as his lips touched hers. "Thanks again for tonight."

"You're welcome," Scarlett said—did she hear breathlessness or had he imagined it? "I want to do it again."

"What part? The dancing? The . . ."

She kissed him quickly once more as footsteps sounded on the stairs. "All of it."

***

Hearing footsteps, Brad turned away, hiding the erection that kept making untimely appearances. "Okay, I'm ready," Scarlett's mom said, appearing back in the room with a purse thrown over her arm. She gazed at Brad. "Shall we?"

With his coat secure, Brad led her mother through the back door. Behind them, Scarlett waved and set the alarm.

"So it was a good night?" Bernadette asked.

The windchill gladly worked like a cold shower. "The ball was fun. I'm sure Scarlett will tell you all about it tomorrow."

"So she had fun?" He heard the worry in Bernadette's voice.

"She did. We danced."

He could literally feel the tension leave Bernadette as she exhaled. "Perfect. I've so wanted her to have fun. To realize her life isn't over. Thank you so much, Brad, for all of this. For taking care of her and letting her live a little.

You helped her save face, and I'll be forever grateful for that."

"I'm glad she's here too. Todd wouldn't want her wallowing."

"No, he wouldn't. He'd want her to move on with her life. Realize that while Colleen is important, she is more than just a mom. That's she's a woman with her own dreams too."

He opened her car door. "Get in and start her up. Your car probably won't even be warm by the time you get home."

"Going," Bernadette said. "Oh, this leather is cold. Luckily I've got heated seats. Will we see you at church Sunday?"

"Probably not," Brad admitted. He'd given up on any kind of faith long ago.

"You sure? You could join us," she offered expectantly. "Go out to a long lunch with us afterward. We'd love to have you."

"Thanks, but I've got a lot of work to finish here. Maybe another time."

He shut the door and watched as she backed up and went down the alley before heading upstairs to his tiny studio. There he stripped off his tux and folded it neatly, readying it for the dry cleaner. He stripped down to nothing, slid underneath the heavy down comforter that kept away any chill. Closed his eyes.

An image of Scarlett laughing floated into the black space behind his eyelids. They'd been dancing, and she'd thrown back her head and waved her hands in the air, fully in the moment. She'd been beautiful. But then to him, she always had been. And when they'd kissed, it had been all he wanted and more. Her breast had fit perfectly in his hand, and he'd felt the rise of her nipple . . . The memory made him turn rock hard, so he touched himself until the need abated and his brain cleared.

Afterward, he lay there staring at the ceiling. He'd held himself aloof for ten years around her, never allowing her to get close. Was this finally their chance? He thought of the first letter Todd had sent him. He'd long ago memorized every word:

> *This is a heavy task to put on a bud, but we've been friends for too long to mince words. I've enclosed a letter for Scarlett. I need you to keep it until she's ready to see it. How will you know? When she finds someone and you think she's falling in love. I don't want her to be alone, but she's always so stubborn. She's too young for me to be the love of her entire life. That wouldn't be fair. As long as I have a piece of her heart, her love will be big enough for her to move on. Yeah, I've been gone too long, and probably haven't been there for her like I should. So she'll need someone to take care of her until she gets on her feet and I need you to do that for me. Then I'll know she'll be in good hands. Get her back to St. Louis where she belongs. You're there, you'll figure out how. Heck, maybe you'll be the one because I know you've always been sweet on her. I'd be okay*

with that, provided you treat her the way she deserves and not like all those other women who've flitted through your life. Who would have thought I'd be the married dude and you the playboy stud? Do me one favor, just make sure any man would be a great dad to my daughter. And don't let Colleen ever go a day without knowing how much I loved her. And stop blaming yourself. My decisions were always my own. Remember that. Todd

Brad replayed the letter in his head. As much as he'd like to stop blaming himself, he hadn't done enough to stop Todd. Sure, Todd had made his own decisions, but Brad could have done more. Should have done more.

Even so, Brad couldn't shed the guilt. If he hadn't come home, if he'd reenlisted, he would have been on that mission instead of a newbie who'd made a critical, rookie mistake. A mistake that had almost killed the entire unit until Todd had sacrificed himself. Brad couldn't shake the feeling that if he'd only been there, maybe he could have stopped it. Changed fate. Maybe died instead, allowing Todd to be home with his beautiful wife and terrific daughter.

The irony was that, in the end, Todd had given Brad his blessing: *maybe you'll be the one.* Tomorrow she'd get the Valentine's Day flowers Brad had sent, along with a stuffed teddy bear for Colleen. Nothing fancy, like a dozen roses, but an arrangement of tulips that she could eventually plant in the garden out back. An "I'm glad you're here" gift.

He was probably the world's biggest fool.

But then he heard her laughing, felt the kiss of her lips, and part of him wanted nothing more than to commit to leaving the past behind. He'd never been afraid of anything before, but then he'd never been playing with his heart either.

Chapter Five

"So have you talked to Brad?" her mother asked two days later. They were in line at Steve's Hot Dogs on Magnolia; Scarlett's dad had stayed behind after Sunday church for a fish fry committee meeting. "Those flowers yesterday were a sweet touch. Live tulips. You'll be able to plant those outside once it gets warmer. I'll show you how if you don't know."

The arrangement had been a totally out-of-the-blue surprise. The front doorbell had shrilled, and outside had been one frazzled delivery driver. He'd asked her name, handed her a large package wrapped in heavy florist paper, and gone back down the front steps. The entire interaction had taken fifteen seconds. She'd torn into the package to find potted tulips and a teddy bear for Colleen. The card had read, *Glad you're here. Happy Valentine's Day. Brad.*

His kindness had bowled her over, for he'd ordered the flowers before they'd even gone on their date. Before they'd kissed. "Colleen loved her bear. I was completely surprised."

"He didn't have to do that."

"No, he didn't." Scarlett stared at the menu board high above the counter. The line moved up a foot. Luckily there were a few more people in front of them, for she had never seen so many choices of hot dogs. Who knew you could top a hot dog with macaroni and cheese? Or baked beans and potato salad?

"So Brad," her mom prompted. "Have you spoken to him since the delivery?"

"No. He worked yesterday and I texted him, but no reply. He must have been busy, and I haven't seen him yet today. I assume he's going to come over later to finish the drywall since he's off."

"Well, be sure you thank him."

"Mom," Scarlett protested. "I'm not ten. I know that. And Colleen already made him a thank-you note and drew him a picture of the tulips."

"Just trying to help." Bernadette could be as stubborn as her daughter, so Scarlett knew from whom she'd inherited the trait.

"Mom, I know you mean well, but let me handle this. We're friends." Scarlett knew the romantic wheels were already turning inside her mom's head, which was a dangerous thing. Brad had already won her mom over, and her mom came from that generation that didn't believe women over twenty should ever be single.

The kiss had rocked her to her core. She'd touched her

puffy lips later that night, as if making sure it hadn't been a dream. She found Brad sexy as hell. Wanted to kiss him again. Although that might be a huge mistake. Where would she live if things turned sour? She'd hardly gotten settled. She didn't want to mess things up.

The line moved forward and when it was their turn, despite all the mouthwatering choices, Scarlett ordered two plain hot dogs and two small bowls of regular old macaroni and cheese.

"Not very adventurous," her mom noted, ordering a bratwurst topped with sauerkraut.

"I'm sure we'll be frequent visitors. Plenty of time to try everything."

They found a table. Squeezed in. Began to eat. "So thanks for going with us to church," her mom said. "Meant a lot to your dad."

Scarlett had debated attending, then caved. In St. Louis, church was the fastest way of meeting new people and getting involved. "I enjoyed seeing everyone. I was surprised how many still live in the neighborhood. Jenni Moore and I keep in touch via Facebook and I'd planned on calling her, but there she was. We made a playdate for next week."

"That's the thing about high school best friends," her mom remarked. "You pick up right where you left off."

"I hope so. Did I tell you I ran into Tommy Rourke at the Mayor's Ball?"

Her mom made a sympathetic noise. "Terrible what happened to his wife. How's he looking?"

"Fine. Said he'd see us at the fish fry next Friday. Our kids are about the same age."

"Really?" Her mom perked up. Sat a little straighter.

"Yes. His son is three," Scarlett replied. She refused to say anything else, for she could tell her mom was adding Tommy to the potential date-my-daughter pool.

"I'm four," Colleen tossed out. She'd made huge headway in her hot dog and wore a small ketchup mustache.

"You are four. Don't forget to wipe your mouth." Colleen grabbed a napkin, complied and waited expectantly. "You got it all," Scarlett said. Colleen gave her a big grin and picked up her spoon for another bite of macaroni.

"So how did Tommy seem? Interested?"

"Friendly?" Scarlett shot back. She shoveled a spoonful of gooey macaroni into her mouth. "Enough matchmaking. I'm not here for a husband."

"Sorry," her mom said. "I just want you to be happy."

"Why isn't Mommy happy?" Colleen asked, her green-eyed gaze turning worried. "Is it because you don't have a prince?"

"Mommies don't need princes to be happy. And I am happy. Very much so."

Colleen didn't look convinced. "Why have you been sad, Mommy? You cried when we left our old house."

"I'm not sad. Sometimes you cry when you leave things." Scarlett was mortified that she'd forgotten little ears were listening yet again. It was like the move had deleted her common sense. "Like I will be somewhat sad when you start full-day preschool next August because that means you are a big, big girl and I will miss you."

"I liked the school when we visited."

"Yes, and we've got a lot of programs to go do at the Carondelet YMCA. Like swimming, ballet and gymnastics. Lots to do." Scarlett's mom inserted herself into the conversation.

"Yay," Colleen said. "That sounds like fun. I like to swim. Just like my daddy."

"Exactly, and don't forget you and I have some grandma dates to plan. And I've found a good mommy's-day-out program too. I'll enroll you next week."

"Will there be kids there?"

"Yes."

"Mom," Scarlett began but Bernadette arched an eyebrow. Scarlett sighed and tuned out of the conversation as her mom and Colleen began to discuss their upcoming activities. Was this what it felt like to be an observer in your own life instead of a participant? She now understood how Cinderella felt the day after the ball. She'd gone from such a high point to back to the same old mundane life. Surely there had to be more to motherhood than scheduling ballet classes? What about her dreams?

Back in San Diego, she'd never noticed how she'd put her life on hold. She'd taken classes toward her bachelor's degree, which she'd stopped once Colleen had come along. But she'd had a role. A place as Todd's wife. Now she was simply Colleen's mom. Not that she didn't love her daughter.

But when Colleen went to school, what then? The thought disconcerted. She had no hobbies. She assumed she could go back to school, could get a job.

She stabbed at her macaroni and cheese, her mother and Colleen still chatting nonstop.

Friday night she'd felt alive. Brad had told her she was beautiful, and kissed her so soundly she'd heated all over. Desire had flickered to life when his full lips had widened into a devastating smile, and passion had flared when those lips had found hers. His touch had sent an awakening tremor through her—one that had let her know that she wasn't emotionally or physically dead. She'd laced her hands around his broad shoulders and laid her head on a solid chest. She'd listed to the beat of his heart. He'd made her feel wanton, yet cherished and safe all at the same time. He was a warrior. A man's man. A protector.

She tuned back in to the conversation. Watched as her mother bowled Colleen over with plans, all great ideas that had Colleen bubbling over with excitement.

At that moment Scarlett realized she was in a funk. She had to get it together. Find a life, so to speak. Do what she wanted to do instead of letting everyone around her decide her future. That was once she figured out what it was.

"Hey, Mom, do you mind if I meet you at Sean's? You could drop me at the house. Take my car and pick me up later. You could take Colleen back with you. Do you want to visit Granny's house?"

Colleen nodded, her mouth full with a final bite of hot dog.

"You don't mind, do you?" Scarlett asked as her mom shook her head. "I have tax paperwork I need to sort through and Colleen will probably have a better time with you than watching a movie."

"I'm going to bake cookies for tonight's dessert. Colleen, would you like to help me with that? Are you good at making chocolate-chip cookies? Because I need an expert."

"Yes!" she enthused. "I've helped Mommy before."

"Then it sounds like we have a plan," her granny said, "because you sound like the expert chef I need to help me."

"I am." Colleen nodded solemnly.

"Are you a good cleaner too? Can you put these things in the trash?"

Colleen's head bobbed again. "Yes."

Scarlett watched as Colleen carefully carried the trash over to the receptacle. "Thanks, Mom. I could use some time to myself. Get some things done."

"Of course," her mom said. She reached out her hand and covered Scarlett's. "That's what I'm here for. Why I wanted you to move home. How about you drop us at my house instead? That way you can have your car and meet us at Sean's later."

Scarlett shook her head. "This way you'll have her car seat. It's too much of a pain to move it. And you have to drive by my house on the way to Sean's anyway."

"If you're sure. Good work, Colleen. You're a great

helper." Colleen beamed from ear to ear at the compliment.

They rose to their feet, and within five minutes Scarlett kissed her daughter good-bye and waved as her Prius disappeared down the alley.

She took a deep breath, inhaled the cold city air. Absorbed the permanent gray sky that seemed to permeate St. Louis this time of year. Scarlett made her way up the back path, inserted her key and opened the door. The alarm beeped once, indicating it was already turned off.

She frowned, then relaxed as she saw Brad's coat tossed over one of the chairs surrounding the island. He must be upstairs working on the third floor. She hung her coat on the peg rack he'd installed and set her purse on the counter. She ascended the back stairs, and because she assumed he was one more floor up, paid little attention to where she was going. With a thump, she ran straight into him as he was exiting the hall bathroom.

"Oh." She stepped backward, and Brad's hands reached out and steadied her before she lost her footing and fell backward down the stairs.

"Careful." He swung her around so she was fully in the hall. A shockwave powered through her. He leaned down and studied her, brown eyes concerned. "You okay?"

She gulped, but no words came out. Brad wore nothing but a white towel slung low over his hips, and it gaped above the knee, giving her a good glimpse of rock-hard thigh. She swallowed as her gaze traced the line of dark hair that made a path from his navel to the towel. A drop of water fell from his tussled hair and slid down his right pectoral. His abs went beyond six-pack. Another clear droplet fell. He'd been in the shower. Gone was the sexy stubble—his clean-shaven face smelled of cypress and eucalyptus.

She brought her gaze back to a face that was watching her intently. "You okay?" he asked again.

"I . . . I . . ." Her mouth dried. She felt fire. She wanted to lick the water from his chest, taste the salt of his skin. Follow that thin little scar over his heart. As if it had a mind of its own, her hand moved to that spot. Touched. Traced. A tremble went through him and his breath hissed. His hand covered hers and drew hers away. "Stop."

"What? Does it hurt?"

His eyes darkened. "No. It's long healed. But you can't touch me like that. I can't hold it together if you do."

"Oh." She absorbed the implications. It was hard to concentrate. His hand held hers. Seeing him wearing nothing but a quick-dry towel fried her equilibrium. His free hand gripped the towel, which tented in front. She wanted that white cloth to fall to the floor, expose what was beneath. Every one of her pores longed for more of his touch. Heat built. Was she wet? Holy hell. She fought for control.

She felt a bit light-headed. Weak at the knees. He must have sensed that, because he immediately let her hand go and snaked that arm around her waist, steadying her. Her hands pressed up against that rock-solid chest. Her legs intertwined with his; she could feel his erection. Her eyes dilated. Oh God. This desire was different from any she'd experienced. The overwhelming urge to have him inside her roared, filling her with pure need.

"You look woozy. Are you getting sick?"

"No." Not unless every one of her dormant hormones powering back to life counted. Her knees buckled.

"Let's get you to the couch." He scooped her up—a rugged male movement that did little to put out the fire. He carried her into the living room and set her on the sofa. "Let me get you some water." He returned a minute later with a tall glass from the kitchen. "Here. Drink up. Where's Colleen?"

"She's with my mom." Scarlett sipped. Stared. No man should be so lethal in a towel. Or so close. If she reached forward she could part the towel. Take him into her mouth and taste him. Swirl her tongue over him and suck. Make him thrust while she cupped his balls. . . . She averted her eyes and dug her fingers into her leg. Listen to her! Who was this woman? When had she gotten so brash? So bold? She hadn't wanted to do that with Todd. Not since . . .

"I'm sorry I scared you. Next time I'll leave a note on the door. Or the counter. I thought you'd be gone all afternoon. When I walked her out the other night, your mom said something about a long lunch."

"We went to Steve's Hot Dogs because my dad had a meeting. Something with the fish fry. I thought I'd spend some time by myself." The tulips were right next to her, beautiful pink blooms with white edges.

"I'm sorry I bothered you. Let me get dressed and get

out of your way."

"You aren't bothering me. I . . ."

"Scarlett."

"I . . ." That new side of her took over. "I want to touch you."

He brushed away a falling droplet. Magnificent hands rubbed into his wet hair, tossing out a light spray. "Scarlett."

"I've thought of nothing since we kissed. I want more."

He glanced toward the spare bedroom, where some of his clothes were hanging in the closet. "We can talk after I get dressed. I'm rather exposed here."

"Do you realize I've never seen another man naked? Do you realize how tempting you are? You make me feel again."

He literally groaned. "Scarlett, I'm standing here in nothing but a towel. Please, I'm going to go get dressed now."

With that he turned, fled to the bedroom and closed the door. Immediately Scarlett felt a letdown. A chill washed over her and her face reddened with shame. What had she been doing? For a seduction, it was terrible. Worse, the minute he'd left, the guilt had crept in.

She couldn't use Brad like this. She couldn't risk losing her place to live, and even more importantly, she couldn't let her integrity slip away. He was pure temptation in the flesh, but just because her ego had been dented, she couldn't use another to massage it back to health. She had to save herself, not wait for one of Colleen's princes. Scarlett sipped more water, not that the liquid calmed her churning insides.

She hadn't felt like a whole woman for a few years. At the end of the last leave, Todd had admitted his guilty secret: that he'd cheated. Oh, just one shore leave and just one blow job, but it had made Scarlett feel like a failure. She hadn't been enough for him. Hadn't been worth waiting for. The revelation had shattered her. Made her question everything, wonder if there had been even more times he hadn't revealed.

Brad returned dressed in a pair of low jeans and a tight T-shirt. He looked at the empty glass. "Is that helping? Are you feeling better?"

"No. And I'm sorry. I shouldn't have come on to you. I'm not sure what came over me. I'd blame stress, but really, I have no excuse." He sat next to her on the sofa, the cushion giving under his weight. "The truth is you made me feel something I hadn't felt in a long time and I took advantage of you and your hospitality."

"Scarlett."

"He cheated on me, you know. He admitted it before he shipped out for the last time." She stared at Brad. "Oh God. You knew."

***

Brad felt the guilt that flashed over his face. He'd been livid when he'd found out what Todd had done. "I told him he was an ass and an idiot. Told him if he did it again, I'd kill him. He wouldn't need to worry about being shot on the front line. Believe me, if I'd been there, I would have stopped him. But I wasn't there."

And the guilt of that continued to eat him alive.

Scarlett's doe eyes blinked. She took a deep inhale. "It hurt, you know. My perfect marriage was a bust. Todd swore it was nothing. Just a physical release. But it hurt. It meant I wasn't good enough."

"You are plenty good enough," Brad ground out. He settled deeper onto the couch beside her.

She peered at him. "Was there more than that one time? I'll never know. But what matters now is that I'm stuck with that event as if it were a thorn in my side. I didn't forgive him before he left. Even if it was wrong, I never had a chance to say I was sorry or that I would forgive him. What must he think of me?" Tears brimmed in her eyes.

"Oh honey, he knew. He knew how much you loved him."

Brad settled her against his chest and she eased into place as if she'd been made for this spot. "You have nothing to feel guilty about. He was secure in your love. He might not have known how to be a stateside Navy man, but he loved you."

She let the tears flow, finally pulling back after she realized she left wet circles on his shirt. She sniffled. "I'm sorry."

He could care less about what he wore. "No biggie.

I've got more clothes."

He held her and let the silence stretch. "How do you do it?" she finally asked.

"Do what?"

"Date? Get back in the saddle. I guess I'm going to have to do that."

The whole idea of her dating anyone but him grated. "There's no rush."

"It's been two years. I have to move on. But if I don't even recognize when someone is flirting with me, how will I survive? I don't understand this Web stuff and I'm not swiping on my phone."

"Dating isn't all it's cracked up to be. I haven't been in the pool in a while."

She lifted her face. "Really? I don't believe that."

"Truth. I haven't . . . uh, been with someone since Todd died."

His words landed like a brick thrown into water. Shock made her mouth widen in disbelief. "No way."

"Yes way. No one has interested me."

"Surely that's not possible. No one?"

He tucked a piece of hair behind her ear. "Well, there is someone. Time will tell if things will work out."

"You're a beautiful man. She's probably a fool. Have you told her how you feel?"

"I think she's figuring it out." The light dawned and Scarlett's lips formed an O. "But it's still pretty early to tell."

"Agreed," Scarlett whispered, absorbing what he'd said.

"Did you feel like you were betraying Todd when you kissed me?"

"No. Did you?"

He shook his head. "But I don't want to ruin our friendship." It was his greatest fear.

"Me either." She shifted. "But I want you to kiss me again. I want to feel like before. See if it's not a fluke caused by some dancing and wine. It feels wrong to ask. So clinical. But it didn't feel that way before."

She paused and blinked. "I can't believe I even said that."

She shifted off his chest, moved a hand to his mouth, and traced his lips with her forefinger. "I want to kiss you again. May I kiss you again?"

"Scarlett," Brad protested.

She sat up and swiveled around so she sat on his lap. She placed her hands on his chest and he sat there like a statue. "You feel fantastic." She traced a line down his neck.

He grabbed her hands then. Pinned her arms to her side. Took her mouth in his and gave her a harsh, aggressive kiss that sent her reeling. His cock jumped to attention. Her breasts felt heavy against him. Then, without freeing her arms, he tore his mouth away. Lifted his head. Spoke.

"I want you. I wanted to drop that towel and bury myself in you. But I want all of you. I am not going to be just a body. You want to kiss me? To make love to you? Then we go on dates. With you it isn't impersonal sex. I have my hand for that."

Scarlett's face revealed she felt the thin veil of control

he had. She pressed a hand to his chest, registering his heaving, uneven breathing. "What are you saying?"

"I've been celibate for three years. I want to be married. Have kids. Be normal. I've liked you since high school. I stayed out of Todd's way because that's the bro code and he was my friend."

"Is that why you never were nice to me."

"It was too hard. I wanted you to much. But I'm not in high school anymore. Neither are you. I'm here for you as a friend, but because I'm older, wiser and maybe somewhat stupid to turn your offer of sex away, I'm saying no. If we're going to be physical, which I would really like, I want more than just the benefits part. I want it all. I'm not settling for anything less."

Her mouth dropped open and he waited on pins and needles. Finally she spoke. "Okay."

He frowned. His forehead creased. "Okay, what?"

"Okay, I agree with you."

She was making no sense. He'd given her a complete out. A way to save face. "I don't understand. Do you agree with me about me wanting it all?"

"Yes, and the part about getting to know each other. You just said that if I wanted sex with you then we were going to get to know each other. I'm agreeing to those terms."

Oh shit. "Scarlett, I . . ."

"No, don't you back out now." She jabbed her finger in his chest. Poked him hard. "I have never been kissed like that. Ever. I'm scared shitless that you and I are going to screw up whatever this is and I'll be out on the street—or worse, back with my mom and dad. But I'm willing to risk it because I'm feeling something I've never felt before. I think about you all the time. You're in my head. I like seeing you and talking to you. I looked forward to all your calls. Did you know that? You would talk and talk, which was great. Even though I never knew you liked the Beatles."

"They are the best."

"U2. Stones. Whatever. When we kiss, it's magical. It's beyond explanation, and it's just a damn kiss. It shouldn't be like this, but it is. So yes. I've been cautious too long. Let's do this."

"It was only a kiss," he lied. He'd never kissed any woman like he kissed her. He could still taste her on his lips. He wanted to kiss her again and not stop.

"Well, if that was just a kiss, I can't wait to see what it's going to be like once we get to know each other better. I felt that kiss in my toes."

"Fine," he replied, for how did you resist the one woman you've always wanted when she agreed to your terms? And he'd felt that kiss in his toes too. And a whole lot of other throbbing places.

"Great. We'll start tonight. You're going to take me to dinner at my brother's."

Hands went up in protest. "Whoa. Slow down. That's a family event."

She turned the full force of those brilliant green eyes on him. Wiggled in his lap. Dared him to contradict. "So? It's food and conversation, which is what you mentioned we needed. I'm not going to play footsie with you under the table and no one will think twice if I bring you along. My mom loves you already. I'll text Maureen and tell her to set an extra plate. Ring the doorbell at five thirty. Unless you have more work to do here?"

"No. That's why I was in the shower." He stared at her, amazed. She was dead serious. "Who are you and what have you done with the old Scarlett?"

"She's gone. I left her in San Diego. This is the new me. See you at five thirty." And with that declaration, Scarlett headed into her bedroom and closed the door.

***

Inside the safety of her room, Scarlett sat on her bed. Waited until the keypad in her bedroom beeped, indicating Brad had left. She pressed a hand to her forehead. She had never been that forthcoming, that aggressive.

Was she crazy? Clearly she'd cracked. The stress of the last two years, coupled with the few before that, must have made her reach her breaking point. Or was this forthright, assertive woman actually the real Scarlett Harrison?

She had no idea. She picked up the phone. Called her sister-in-law and asked her if Brad could tag along. No explanation was necessary or given, and as expected, Maureen agreed. Scarlett glanced at the clock. She had a couple of hours to kill. She wandered into her en suite bathroom. She'd pulled her hair into a tight bun for church, and now she pulled out the holder and let the golden strands fall to her shoulders. Growing up she'd hated how pale her hair was—almost white. She'd felt a bit freakish and burned instead of tanning. Todd had told her she was pretty, and she'd latched on, marrying her high school sweetheart. She'd felt pretty and desired the other night in Brad's arms, felt cherished when the tulips are arrived. She finished her business. Washed her hands.

She walked out into the living room. She should unpack the last few boxes. Instead she turned on the TV and found the Hallmark Channel. How long had it been since she'd sat on her couch and watched something other than a Disney movie? How many times had she watched the prince rescue the princess?

Brad was a special guy, and she wanted him. Tommy might have been flirting, but she'd felt no flicker of interest toward Sean's friend. Not like how the room seemed to light up the moment Brad entered. She touched one of the tulip petals. Then she took a forefinger and touched her puffy lips. No, she'd never been kissed so soundly, as if she couldn't tell where her mouth stopped and his began. For the first time in several years, a sense of hope flickered and bloomed. Time for this princess to take charge and rescue herself.

Chapter Six

Sean and Maureen lived in a converted two-family building on Columbia, in a part of St. Louis called the Hill. "Hey Brad, good to see you," Sean greeted as he opened the door.

"I hope I'm not intruding."

"Nah. The more the merrier. Glad you joined us." Brad put his hand on the small of Scarlett's back, guiding her as they stepped inside, his touch reminding her of being in his arms earlier.

Everyone crowded on the first floor; what used to be a three-room shotgun flat had been gutted into an open-concept living room, dining room and kitchen combination. Colleen's cousin Rory was six and her cousin Eileen was eight. At age two, Mary toddled after all of them as they raced and shrieked throughout the house. "Upstairs!" Maureen yelled, and four pairs of children's feet pounded their way to the second floor, where the bedrooms were.

"The munchkins are noisy," Maureen said, carrying a bowl of Italian salad, which she set on the dining room table. She put down a pair of tongs and gave Scarlett an air kiss. "So good to see you. Glad you're finally back. We are going to have such fun."

"Is there anything I can do to help?" Scarlett asked.

Maureen waved her aside. "Just pour yourself a glass of wine and make sure you top mine off too. Long weekend. I deserve it."

"You sure do, hon," Sean said, dropping a kiss on her lips. "Brad, want a beer?" Sean called.

"Love one," Brad said. "Thanks."

"Maureen always makes plenty." Bernadette put a baking sheet covered with cheesey garlic bread on the dining table. "Hope you like lasagna."

"Love it," Brad replied, his mouth watering. "Been awhile since I've had a home-cooked meal, aside from those pork chops the other night."

"Well, this isn't the stuff you pull out of the freezer either," Sean said, handing him a can of Busch beer. "My wife can cook."

"Do you cook?" Brad asked Scarlett as she returned from the kitchen area carrying a very generous glass of red wine.

"Not like Maureen," she admitted.

"No one cooks like my wife," Sean bragged. "Her parents own . . ." He named an Italian eatery a few blocks over. "It's where we met. She was waiting tables. I was actually there on a double date. I went back the next night to ask her out."

Brad hadn't known that. "Love that place."

"Well, this is my family's secret recipe," Maureen said, carrying in a steaming pan. Gooey cheese had melted all over the top.

"That smells delicious," he complimented.

She gave Brad a warm smile. "It's going to be yummy. Go call the urchins," she prompted her husband.

"Even though you literally just sent them upstairs?" Sean asked.

Maureen puckered her lips and shot him a look down her nose, and soon everyone sat around the table, even Mary, who still used her high chair. Scarlett's dad, James, said grace, and everyone dug in.

"So, Brad, how did you spend your Valentine's Day?" Maureen asked as she served the lasagna.

Brad accepted the plate being passed to him. "Actually, I worked. My crew went door-to-door, checking on people and installing smoke detectors or replacing the batteries."

"Oh, I saw that story," Bernadette said. She sat down, all the kids now with plates. "That was your firehouse?"

"One of them. Other houses worked the parade and there were a few fires, but nothing major. The department does community outreach and each time we do, it always amazes me how many people still don't have working detectors."

"Well, no worries here," Sean said. "My cousin Bernie's an electrician and he hardwired them in."

"What's hardwired?" Eileen asked.

"Means they all go off at once when one senses smoke," Sean told his daughter.

"Very safe. They're code now and installed in my house," Brad added.

"He's a fireman," Colleen told her older cousin.

"Oh." Eileen sized Brad up. "So you save people in fires?"

"That's one part of my job," Brad told her.

She seemed skeptical. "So you really have?"

"Yes," Brad told her.

"He's also a prince," Colleen inserted, not to be left out, "because we live in a castle. You can come over and see it."

"I want to see it," Rory shouted. "Princes have swords and fight dragons. Do you have a dragon?"

"No dragons." Scarlett laughed. "And you can all see it."

As the conversation took off in a different direction, Scarlett relaxed. By the end of dinner, plates were polished clean and everyone was full. "I'm going to have to run for a week," Sean complained. He glanced at Brad. "Don't even say it. You're already too darn fit for this family."

"Only because I'm training to do the Fight for Air climb," Brad said.

Scarlett frowned. "What's that?"

"It's a fund-raiser for the American Lung Association. I'll be climbing all forty floors of Metropolitan Square at the end of March. I'm on a first responders' team. Our goal is to raise a couple thousand dollars."

"Sounds like a noble cause," Bernadette said.

Impressed, Scarlett raised her wineglass in a silent toast. He was more than a great kisser. She discovered something new every day that raised him in her esteem. He responded with a lift of his eyebrows. Then he took another swig of his beer. "Do you still swim, Sean?"

"Not as much as I'd like. You?"

"I try to hit the pool at least three times a week. But remember I'm out on the Mississippi for the fire department. So I have to stay in shape. I'd hate to be on call and not be strong enough. That river is swift."

Maureen giggled. "You have no worries. I saw that calendar. You're in pretty good shape."

"Maureen," Scarlett's mom chided. "Don't embarrass your guest."

"Sorry," Maureen said, but her subsequent giggle indicated she had no shame. Sean simply rolled his eyes, a trait he'd learned from his father. He knew what he'd married. Knew he had nothing to worry about. "So are you part of the bachelor auction too?" Maureen asked.

"What auction?" Bernadette said. She looked at Brad.

"The one to find the next group of calendar guys," Brad said. "Given the popularity of the calendar, the committee decided that it would take the thirty most eligible public servants and put them up for auction. The ones who earn the most money will be in the calendar. It's all for charity, and no, thankfully I'm done with all that. I have to make an appearance, but I'm not up for sale.

Another guy in my house is, though."

"Too bad," Maureen said mischievously. "I'd buy you for Scarlett."

"Maureen!" both Scarlett and her mother said at the same time.

"What?" She shrugged, not at all ashamed. "It's for charity. And you went with him to the ball. I'm sure he'd rather have you win him than some crazy woman who really wants to see what's under that Speedo."

"I was not wearing a Speedo," Brad said.

"Oh, with the amount of muscled skin, I must not have noticed," Maureen said, reaching for her wine, wicked smirk clearly in place. "Just regular old swim trunks then?"

Scarlett's face had flamed bright red. She'd almost seen what was under that swimsuit, and would have if Brad hadn't kept a grip on the towel. And who knew her sister-in-law was such a shit disturber.

"You okay, Scarlett?" Maureen asked. "You look a little flushed."

"Fine," Scarlett replied, reaching for her wine. "I'm just fine. Wine does this to me. It's my pale skin."

Scarlett saw Brad's eyebrow lift at her lie.

"Had to make sure. Okay, everybody, we have cookies and ice cream for dessert." Maureen changed the subject and her demeanor. "Who wants some? Who's not too full?"

"Me!" the kids chorused.

"I helped Granny make the cookies," Colleen announced proudly. "They're chocolate chip."

"Then I definitely want some dessert," Scarlett's dad

announced.

"Me too," Brad said. "They're my favorite." He winked at Scarlett, indicating he knew she'd been blushing because of what had happened between them.

"Me three," Scarlett added, desperate to get her heart rate under control. All he had to do was smile and she melted. She felt sorry for all those women who'd lusted after him. She now understood their pain.

"Cookies and ice cream for everyone," Bernadette announced. She stood up and followed Maureen into the kitchen area. "I'll come help you," she offered, and Scarlett knew her sister-in-law was about to get an etiquette lecture, or as much of one as her mother could give with the kitchen open to everyone.

"Cookie," Mary said as her mom went by.

"Don't worry, pumpkin. I won't forget your cookie," Maureen replied, ruffling her daughter's hair. She grinned at Scarlett.

And with that, things went back to normal, with no more mention of Brad or anything to do with the calendar. Scarlett polished off her wine—one glass was enough. She had to drive later. Until then, she wanted to enjoy the night and watch Brad interact. He fit right in. Seemed like he was having fun. Well, he'd wanted to get to know her. This was it. Her crazy family. Take it or leave it.

"Hey, I wanted to say thanks for tonight," he told her later as he walked Scarlett to the back door. She carried Colleen, who'd fallen asleep. "I had a great time."

"You didn't find us too overwhelming? Maureen went

after you about your swimsuit."

He chuckled. "Nah. Dinner was nice. My family isn't nearly as rambunctious. We argue politics and get into heated debates about how Congress is inept. I liked playing Chutes and Ladders. Seriously. Made for a nice change of pace. Here, let me."

He unlocked the door and opened it. He stepped inside first and turned off the alarm as she carried her daughter inside. "Sleepy," Colleen mumbled as Scarlett removed her daughter's parka. Brad shed his and tossed it on a bar stool. "Here, let me take her," he said. "She looks heavy."

"Well, you're the super-fit one." Scarlett passed Colleen over.

"Ha-ha. Funny."

"Please," Scarlett teased. "I know exactly what I saw and felt today. Don't try to hide it now."

She led him upstairs. Turned on Colleen's night light. Pulled back the covers on her bed. Brad held Colleen while Scarlett removed her daughter's socks and shoes.

Brad set her gently on the bed and drew up the covers. "She's completely out."

"She had a busy day. Cooking with her grandma and then running crazy with all her cousins. We haven't had that in a long time. She's never played with her cousins."

They watched Colleen sleep for a few minutes to make sure she stayed asleep. "You didn't come home once, did you?"

"No. My parents visited, but I never brought Colleen

back. We rarely traveled. Well, up to Disney. Sea World. Airfare's expensive and I wanted to leave St. Louis in the past. I'm not sure why. I guess I just had these big dreams, and really, aside from being a mom, they didn't work out. I didn't want to have people here thinking I was a failure."

"You're not a failure. You're a fantastic mother and isn't that the most important job?"

"Yes, but who am I then without Colleen? You're a firefighter. You save people. I, well, I don't know what I am."

"I think you're enough exactly how you are."

"Really?" She assessed him. "You're just saying that because you're my friend."

"I'm saying it because it's true." He followed her out into the upstairs living area. She pulled the door partially closed.

"Thank you for going tonight."

"I had fun." He paused. "Did I pass your test?"

He reached for her and drew her into his arms. Pulled her close and wrapped his arms around her. "Did I pass yours?" she asked.

"Absolutely." He captured her mouth with his. At first the kiss was simple. A little press. Then tiny nips and tugs. Scarlett opened her mouth wider and sucked his lip inside, at which his lips became more insistent. This time he branded her, sealed her to him. His fingers cupped her chin, and tilting her face so he could kiss her even deeper, he explored every little crevice with his tongue. When they came up for air, Scarlett's skin was on fire, and he ran his lips down her neck to the collar of her shirt. Her breasts ached, wanted him to touch them. "More," she breathed, her voice deep and throaty. "Touch me. Please."

She again felt the tip of his tongue trace her mouth before he plunged inside, making her hot and needy. She ran her fingers into his hair and brought his head even closer to hers. He wove his leg between hers, cupped her backside, pulling her against his erection. She made a tiny noise in the back of her throat. Reached for his shirt. Tugged it from the waistband and found his chest with her palms. His breath hitched, and his hands found the hem of her shirt and yanked it. Her arms flew up and her shirt went upward, and Brad's mouth found her left breast through the lace of her bra. Scarlett's head fell back as he drew the fabric-covered mound inside and sucked. Her legs shook. So, she ground on him, trying to assuage the need he'd built. She needed to come. She brought her lips to his collarbone, kissed his skin as he moved the fabric aside and took her fully into his warm mouth. "Oh God." She'd never been so wet, so . . . Her body shook. His hand twirled her other nipple, the one not plundered by his tongue. She felt the orgasm arrive, pushed herself harder against him and her body let go. "Oh, oh, oh . . ." she cried, not caring how wanton and needy she sounded as her body quaked. She trembled. She grabbed for his shirttail again. "I want you inside me."

But he was putting her bra to rights and pulling her shirt back down. "Not tonight."

Her breath came in slow pants. "What?"

"I want you. But not tonight."

She suddenly felt foolish. "Why not?"

He jerked a hand through his hair. "I don't want to rush. Neither of us has had sex in a while. I don't want to be focused only on physical release. Two dates do not make a relationship. Sex should be a destination, not a distraction."

Her heated body protested, but her heart and head knew he was right. "Then when will I see you again?"

"I'm working tomorrow and then I'm off until Saturday. We can plan something. My only agenda was to paint the third floor."

"I can help with that. I painted my house in San Diego."

"I may take you up on that offer."

She placed her hand on his arm, needing to stay connected. "Please do. All I'm doing this week is helping to bake desserts for the fish fry. I can't cook like Maureen, but I can make a cake."

"So this fish fry is a big deal? I mean, I know St. Louis goes crazy over fish fries, but I've never been."

She nodded. "It is. I grew up with them. If you go, I'll serve you dessert." She gave him a shy smile. Got bolder. "Maybe even save you some icing that you could put on me in creative places afterward."

His face split into a smile, reassuring her all was okay. "Oh, for that I'll definitely go. But I have to be honest with you. I've already been recruited to help out. Your dad hit me up. I'm now on the fry committee. What about firefighter says I wanted to be in a kitchen with a wire basket going into heated oil?"

She laughed. "Uh-oh. You're a fry cook. You realize that once you're in, you'll never leave? You're stuck for life. You'll really need me to cover myself in icing after that."

He grinned. "Then maybe it'll be worth it."

The tension left her somewhat as they flirted. "Have to take the good with the bad."

He reached for her then, drew her to his body and pressed her against him. "Well, I can tell you'll be very, very good."

His lips hovered above hers, so close he could capture her breath. He kissed her again, and then drew away with a groan. "I have to go." He put a finger on her lips. Traced the outline of her mouth. Her lips felt full and puffy. Bereft. Her hands pressed against his chest, wanting to undo the buttons holding the chambray placket closed. She could probably tempt him to stay. She reached for a button. She was okay with some fast-forward.

Brad caught her fingers. "No. Not tonight. When we make love, it will change everything. And we can't go back from it. And trust me, what I plan to do to you will take all night. I'm going to put you on your back and have my wicked way with you until all you can do is make those delightful little noises from how good it is and scream my name."

She quivered. Wanted that now. Instead, he leaned down and branded her with a kiss on the cheek. "If you need me, text. If not, I'll catch up with you sometime on

Tuesday. I'll try to call. Stay out of trouble until then."

"Okay."

"I'll lock up. You can stay up here."

"Okay," she parroted, and less than a minute later she heard the security system arm itself. She went into her bathroom and readied for sleep. Then she tossed on a large T-shirt and climbed into bed. The light from the streetlamp cast a glow around the edges of the heavy curtains. She'd wanted him. He made her hot and needy. And look how good he'd been with Colleen tonight. He was the full paradoxical package of steamy sex and reliable responsibility.

But he was right. Making love would change things. He'd used the word *relationship*. That this would not be friends with benefits. Oh, she'd wondered if she'd ever find Mr. Right a second time. Liked the idea, but wasn't actively looking. She wanted to experience adult passion and desire—all those things she'd missed out on by marrying so young.

Heck, her first sexual experience had been in the backseat of Todd's car. Her next a quickie in his bed one Saturday afternoon when his parents had been out. Sure, sex had gotten better, but she wanted her body to sing as if it was a finely tuned instrument played under master tutelage. Brad clearly knew his way around a woman's body. She wanted him to show her what she'd been missing all these years.

If that meant she had to agree to his terms, then for now she was more than willing. He had four days off starting on Tuesday. She planned on taking advantage of all of those.

***

Despite Scarlett's best intentions to spend time with Brad, her mother had other ideas. Tuesday, Scarlett went to the YMCA and signed Colleen up for a variety of classes and activities, including Mommy's Day Out. Wednesday her mother had her at the church, helping prepare the homemade side items for the fish fry. That meant Scarlett found herself with the delightful job of peeling endless bags of potatoes, all of which would become potato salad once cooked. Colleen didn't mind—she ran around and played with kids her age. Most kids were with their grandmothers, so that didn't help Scarlett meet anyone her age. Thursday, she was back at church, baking and icing sheets of cake. Then there was the job of cutting the cake into individual portions, putting it on the china plates, and wrapping the iced slices with plastic wrap to keep everything fresh. Not only was there cake, but pie covered in meringue. She cut and wrapped it all. "This is almost like having a full-time job," she told her mother.

"And you were worried you'd be sitting at home," her mom replied. "I told you I'd keep you busy. Tomorrow you can take a break during the day. Just be here no later than three thirty. We open at four and we'll have a line by five. Unless you want to also be here Friday morning to bread the fish?"

"I'll pass," Scarlett said. "I've really got some things I want to do."

Like seeing Brad. They'd spoken briefly on the phone and swapped a few texts, but she hadn't been in the same room with him, which was why at nine a.m. Friday, Scarlett was waiting on pins and needles on her couch when she heard the alarm beep and Brad make his way up the back stairs. She rose quickly. "Hey, can I help?" she called.

"Are you actually here today?" he asked as he reached the landing.

She met him on the stairs. "Amazingly enough, yes. I escaped my mom's plans to bread fish."

He grinned. "And you swapped that for painting?"

"Yes. I don't want to be up to my elbows in fish stuff. Besides, I said I would and I wanted to see you."

"Me too, and you know I'd love your help."

"I'll let Colleen know where I'll be and meet you up there."

A few minutes later, Scarlett gasped as she entered the front room, the one Brad was making into a playroom. "I really should be checking your work every day. I can't believe how much progress you've made." Already the ceiling was painted white. The built-ins were white, and the walls a perfect shade of pale pink.

"Thanks." Brad wore a pair of carpenter whites and a tight white T-shirt, both covered with white and pink paint splatters. The splotches only heightened his appeal. Muscles bulged as he poured pink paint into a tray. "This is the last coat. I noticed Colleen liked pink. Wanted this room to be perfect for her."

"This is going to be beautiful. She's going to love it." What he'd done touched her.

"I've got furniture on order from Pottery Barn, including a big area rug and a table and chairs from their kids catalog and a small modular seating unit from their teen catalog."

Scarlett stared at him. "Brad, this is too much. You didn't have to do this."

"I wanted to." He handed her a two-inch angled brush, fingers touching as he transferred it into her hand. "I need you to cut in so I can roll the paint on."

He'd taped off the baseboards with green frog tape and she bent down and began to paint a strip. "There's a stool over there. Can you reach the top of the wall?" he asked.

"Yeah," she said.

He'd covered the wood floor with drop cloths, which was good because occasionally pink paint dripped off her brush. He'd given her a red Solo cup filled with paint, making the process easier as she moved along. Behind her, she heard the smushing sound of the paint roller as it covered the walls.

"So tell me more about you," Scarlett said, squatting to work her way into a corner.

"Like what?"

She glanced over her shoulder. He was rolling up close to the ceiling. "I don't know. We had all those conversations, and yet all I feel like I know about you is that you like the Beatles and biographies. What's something people don't know about you?"

Brad groaned. Biceps bulged as he reached the pole toward the ceiling and rolled it up and down. "Great. Start with a hard one."

"Okay, well, try this. How did you learn how to do all this work?"

"Helping a buddy out. Most firefighters have a side job. I'm not musical, but I am good with my hands." Up and down. Back and forth. He moved in perfect rhythm as he painted, his hands clasped around the extension pole, proving he was definitely good with his hands. Who knew painting could be so sexy? He dipped the roller in the pan. Returned to the wall.

"Also my dad taught me," Brad continued. "He and my mom rehabbed my childhood home on Flora while I was growing up and my brothers and I helped. Have you been there?"

"Once. Prom. Remember? We met at your house. You took Sylvia something or other. Your parents hosted us for appetizers and photos."

"Oh yeah. I'd forgotten we were there. Haven't looked at those photos in years. I think my parents still have them somewhere. And it was Sylvia Smith. She went to Nerinx."

"I remember she didn't know any of us. And she was all over you."

Brad grinned. "Yeah. Well . . ." He broke eye contact and dipped the roller into the tray. "Can't help that."

"Were you avoiding me then?"

"Yes. She was a nice distraction. I knew Todd was going to ask you to marry him." He returned to painting, changing subjects before she could question him further. "But anyway, I'm the youngest, so I had to learn fast so I didn't get left out. My family's a bit hands-off in the affection department, so working together was our bonding time."

"Oh. No wonder why dinner with my family was so different."

"Not that my childhood was bad," he added with a quick shake of his head. "My dad brewed beer for AB. Union guy all the way. But he's quiet and unassuming. Our house was his piece of paradise, a gift to my mom who stayed home and raised four kids. We were her full-time job. By prom, the house was done and my dad took up fishing instead. He bought a small cabin out on the upper Meramec River out by Sullivan. Fixed that up. Figures they may retire out there someday, although I kind of doubt it because they like the city too much. It's pretty out there, though. A good escape."

"Sounds nice."

"Once the weather gets warmer, I'll take you out there if you'd like. The water is crystal clear and there's some sandy beaches. Onondaga Cave also has tours. So does Meramec Caverns. We can call and find out if Colleen's old enough." He rolled more color on the walls. "Just so you know, Colleen's part of the deal in getting to know you. She's an awesome kid."

His thoughtfulness touched her, just as it had when

he'd sent the teddy bear along with the flowers. "Thanks, it sounds like a great outing once the weather gets nicer. She'll love it."

"Caves are the same temperature all year around."

"I did not know that. Well, I learned something new today. Oh, and I need more paint."

"Bring the cup here."

As she handed him the red cup, the pink paint she'd dripped down the side covered his fingertips. "Oh, I can't believe I did that. Sorry!"

He wiped the paint on his white carpenter pants. "No big deal." He filled her cup back up. "Let's get this finished."

About an hour later they were finished painting. Colleen had checked on them, oohed and ahhed over the pink color, made a few swipes on the wall with a brush, and then gone back downstairs again as her toys were much more entertaining. "Looks great," Scarlett said, putting her cup down on the drop cloth. She faced him, paintbrush dangling. "What?" she asked.

"You have paint on your nose."

She instinctively reached up and rubbed her nose. Pink paint now coated her fingers.

"Here. Let me." Brad took the edge of his shirt and lifted. His torso exposed, he stepped into her space. Used the hem to wipe off the paint. "It's latex. It comes right off."

He rubbed again. Dropped his shirt and put two forefingers in his mouth. Licked them, and then rubbed her nose again. Grabbed his shirt and wiped again. "All gone."

She stared at him wide eyed, her mouth slightly open. Never had a gesture been so innocent, yet so intimate. "Th-th-thanks."

He winked at her, the edges of his lips curling up into a slight smile. "No problem." He crooked a finger and lifted her chin until her jaw closed. Chuckled. "There you go. Don't want you catching flies."

She sputtered. "I can't believe you did that!"

His brown eyes twinkled. "You had paint on your nose. Had to help out."

"You know exactly what I meant." Her hand realized it held a paintbrush. Realized she couldn't let him win this round. "Maybe you should clean this next."

Her arm arched and she swiped the paintbrush along his jawline. "Oh, now it's my turn to say I don't believe you did that," Brad said. She noted he wasn't angry. More amused than disbelieving. Mischievous. His grin widened as he palmed his face, coming away with a handful of paint. He promptly wiped it across her cheek.

"Hey!" she shouted.

"Look, that mouth of yours is open again."

"You . . ." She flicked the paintbrush, flinging pink droplets over his white shirt.

"Uh-oh. Now you've done it. You forget, I was a SEAL. Can't go down without a fight." He captured her hand before she could fling more paint. Ran his free hand over the paint on her cheek and wiped it down her neck.

In turn, she released her fingers, sending the brush to

the cloth below as she smeared more paint on him, until the other side of his face was pink as well. "Bring it on. Unless you want to call a truce. I'd say we're even."

He used a finger and painted the dip between her collarbones. "Maybe now we are."

She made another swipe. Laughed. "Not even close." Reached up to swipe again. He grabbed her wrist.

"You're going to pay for that," he warned.

She liked playing with fire. "Yeah, right. I'm not afraid."

"You should be." He stripped the T-shirt off. Revealed his sculpted chest. She wiggled her fingers, trying to reach him. "Oh, believe me. You'll pay."

She laughed. Got loose and reached down for the paintbrush. But he grabbed her by the waist. Pulled her toward him and spun her around. "Ooh, now I'm scared," she teased. "Got me. What you gonna do next?"

"This," Brad said, bringing his lips down on hers. Perhaps it was static buildup, but an electric shock powered through her the moment his mouth found hers. She heated. Desire shot to her toes, the painting game forgotten. Instead mouths molded together. Fused. He slid his arms farther around her waist, pressed her up against him. His hands slid lower, cupped her bottom. Her hands slid around his neck, fingertips caressing the bare skin of his broad shoulders.

Her tongue slid along his lips, made him open for her so she could explore. She wanted to taste him, to drink him in until she had her fill. Although with a kiss like this, you could never get enough. It swept you away, for as passionate as the kiss was, there was also an underlying tenderness. This softness washed over Scarlett. Took her to that parallel universe where you believed anything was possible. A kiss that didn't scream "let's have sex," but instead was a destination in itself.

She could feel his erection. His desire matched the ache between her legs. He broke off the kiss, sent his lips down the side of her neck that wasn't painted pink. Blazed a trail, for she'd never wanted anyone more. Her skin tingled everywhere he touched.

"Mommy?"

Like a bucket of cold water descending, hearing her name had Scarlett pulling back, turning away as reality intruded. She could hear footsteps. "Mommy? I'm hungry." Colleen appeared in the doorway. She frowned. Pointed at them. "Why do you have paint all over?"

"We spilled some," Scarlett lied. Behind her, Brad yanked his shirt back on and began to clean up the mess they'd made.

"I'm done playing," Colleen announced.

"I'll make you some lunch." She turned back to Brad. Mouthed the word, "Sorry."

"I've got this," he told her, waving her onward. "Go."

"Can I make you some lunch too?" she asked. He'd already put his back to her.

"Sure," he called over his shoulders. "Let me clean this up and I'll be down."

"Okay." She guided Colleen down to the kitchen.

"What were you doing?" Colleen asked as they went to the kitchen.

"Painting."

"You're wearing a lot." Colleen pointed to the spots all over her mom's shirt. "You always tell me to be careful. Why weren't you careful?"

Because Brad is the sexiest man alive and I wanted to feel every inch of him.

"Did you like the color? Brad is making you a pink playroom. How about spaghetti for lunch?"

"I like pink. And spaghetti."

"Go get a box of noodles while I clean up."

Scarlett went to the half bath and shook her head as she saw herself in the mirror. Her lips were puffy from being kissed. Her face and neck were covered in paint. She ran warm water and scrubbed her face. The latex paint peeled off, and after using a little soap, her arms were also clean. When she stepped out into the kitchen, Colleen had retrieved a box of spaghetti noodles and a jar of sauce. "Ready, Mommy."

"Good girl for waiting," Scarlett complimented. She retrieved a four-quart saucepan, filled it with water and set it on the stove she'd finally mastered. By the time Brad came downstairs, a meatless sauce was simmering and the noodles were ready.

"We made spaghetti," Colleen told him. "And I helped."

"You did, huh? You're turning into a great helper." He'd cleaned up, including washing away all the paint. She could tell where it'd been, for his skin was still red in those areas.

By the end of the meal, Colleen wore a ring of spaghetti sauce around her mouth.

"Very good," Brad told them as he put his empty plate in the dishwasher, but Scarlett noticed the smile he gave them didn't create those little crinkles around his eyes.

"Everything okay?" she asked.

"Fine," Brad told her, "but I've got to run. I'll see you later at the fish fry."

"Okay," Scarlett said. She watched him go. Frowned.

"You okay, Mommy?" her observant daughter asked. "Your happy face is upside down."

"Nothing's wrong. I just have all these dishes to do."

"I'll help. Brad said I'm a good helper."

"And you are, so let's get started." Afterward, Scarlett decided, she was marching across the backyard to find out exactly what was going on.

**

After leaving Scarlett's, Brad unlocked the door to his garage studio. Went inside. Closed the door and leaned against it. Laced his fingers atop his head and bent it toward his chest. Stayed there for a minute or two before changing shirts. He wasn't surprised to hear a knock a bit later.

"What's wrong?" she demanded after he let her in.

He'd been eating spaghetti. Colleen had it smeared all

over her face. Scarlett had been laughing. Watching them, the food had become cardboard in his mouth and suddenly tasted like sandpaper. The entire scene had been one of domestic tranquility. Normality. Like they were parents who'd sneaked off for sex while the kids were oblivious.

And that normalcy had scared him more than any war zone ever had. Scared him more than taking on Somali pirates. How could a four-year-old with a face full of food bring a man to his knees? But she had.

Kissing Scarlett had been enjoyable. Extremely pleasurable. Thinking about making love to her made him hard. He wanted her more than any other woman. Always had.

"Brad?" She touched his arm and that was enough. The bed was ten feet away. He could lay her on it and lose himself. Slake this lust. Peel back that layer. Yet he knew better.

Today the idle chatter of a four-year-old as she rambled on about this and that had made him realize how much he had at stake. Scarlett was in full rebound mode. She was stretching her wings and learning to fly. She was turning into a sensual woman who desired sex, specifically sex with him.

But what then? What came next? He'd told her making love would change things. He'd meant for her. But today at lunch he'd realized that it would change things for him as well.

What if afterward Scarlett decided it was just sex? That sex was all she wanted from him? That she'd never see Brad as a man who could fit into her world as a partner, her other half? The stakes had suddenly gotten very high.

"I'm sorry," he told Scarlett.

"Sorry?"

"I . . ." He jerked a hand through her hair. Wondered if kissing her would taste like a mixture of cola and spaghetti sauce. She'd skipped the cookie Colleen had had for dessert. "I'm fine. I can't explain. Please don't ask me to try."

She sized him up, that all-seeing green gaze traveling head to toe. "Okay," she said, reinforcing she'd been married to Todd. Military men had secrets. Their wives and girlfriends learned to back down when their men indicated they couldn't explain, and Scarlett followed suit. "I don't want to leave Colleen alone for very long and I left a mess in the kitchen."

He nodded. "I'll see you tonight at the fish fry. Things will be fine by then. I'm just tired. Maybe inhaled too many paint fumes."

"I'm going to drive separately if that's okay. In case I have to take Colleen home early."

"Okay. Sounds good." He nodded again. He must appear like one of those damn annoying bobble heads. She went out the door. Closed it behind her.

Brad slumped down onto the hard wooden chair that accompanied his tiny table. Bent over and put his head back in his hands. She was the one who'd gotten away, and now he had this second chance. They'd shared so much over the phone, and kissing her had cemented his feelings.

What would he do if she rejected him?

He couldn't imagine losing her and Colleen. Now that he'd spent even more time with her—sex aside—he knew she was the woman of his dreams. The one he wanted to spend the rest of his days with. Maybe he should share the letters early. Take that guilty weight off his chest. Todd wouldn't be here to know Brad hadn't followed his last wishes exactly. Although that would mean compromising his honor. Brad reached for a beer, not caring that it was noon. It was Friday. It was five o'clock somewhere.

And by God, he needed to get ahold of himself before he had fish to fry.

And Scarlett to face.

Chapter Seven

During his time with the SEALs, Brad had been all over the world. After drinking his beer and taking a much-needed, hour-long nap, he'd felt better. More in control. Resolved to do the right thing. But as he walked into Singler Hall, otherwise known as the church basement, all that newfound calm and determination vanished. He'd never seen anything quite like a St. Pius fish fry, and he felt like, to excuse the terrible pun, a fish out of water.

Immediately he could tell the event worked like a well-oiled machine. Eight dollars bought you fish, three sides and dessert. Or four dollars bought a smaller size: half a fish portion and two sides. Clearly half the allure of the fish fry was as a social event, the line snaking through the hallway for "eating in" was much longer than those "carrying out."

For those dining in, dinner was served on china plates. Catholic nuns, not wearing habits, worked the bar, selling soda, and for those twenty-one and older, two-dollar beers.

Kids ran around freely—weaving in and out of the long tables and metal folding chairs, all watched by the entire community. He saw Colleen racing around with her cousins.

He gave a second glance to the sign reading, MAY COD HAVE MERCY ON YOUR SOLE, passed as he walked toward the fry room. He'd been put on fry duty, something he hadn't done since working at McDonald's during high school. Into bubbling hot oil went a wire basket full of freshly breaded fish. Out came fish a crisp, golden brown color. In the kitchen, church members removed baked fish from industrial ovens. Steam tables kept things hot and fresh. No reheated fish here.

The event ran from four to seven thirty, so it was around seven by the time Scarlett's dad told Brad he could go. "We're done cooking," he said. "You did good. Go get yourself a plate."

"Thanks." Brad took off his white apron, put it in the laundry bin, and headed out to the line. He'd learned any extra food was donated to a local soup kitchen, who would use it to feed the homeless. He went through the line, choosing baked fish, green beans, potato salad, applesauce, and a dinner roll. He stopped by the dessert table.

"Hey." Scarlett gave him a megawatt smile that heated him more than standing over the hot fryer had. She'd tamed her hair into a tight knot at the base of her neck. The standard white apron covered jeans and a long-sleeve, scooped-cut T-shirt.

"How's it going?" he asked, wincing because he

sounded so lame. After his nap, he'd seen things clearer. Realized that maybe he was expecting too much from himself, that it was okay not to have all the answers. After all, for a man who could snap his fingers and have women fall at his feet, what he knew about serious relationships wouldn't fill a teacup.

She appeared happy to see him, and he relaxed somewhat. She gestured to the once-full table. "You're down to a choice of cake or pie."

"What do you recommend?"

She pointed. Gave him another smile that tugged at something deep inside. "I've heard the lemon meringue pie's really good. It's been our top pick."

"Pie it is."

"Take this one. It's bigger." She chose a plate and their fingers touched. Again he felt a little zing, a tiny jolt. He wanted to tell her. Knew he couldn't without breaking his promise. "I'll catch up with you in a bit," she told him as someone else approached.

Balancing the plate and cake, Brad went to the bar. Opted for cola instead of beer since he wanted his wits about him. Besides, he was working in the morning and he was already plus one on the day.

He saw Scarlett's brother and Sean waved him over. Pointed to the spot across from him. "I'm on kid duty," Sean relayed as Brad set his food down and yanked out the metal folding chair. Sean pointed to his kids and Colleen. "They'll sleep well tonight."

The house band was playing, and twelve kids filled the

dance floor. The younger ones bent their knees and jumped. The toddlers often wiggled from side to side, shaking their hips as if they were practicing a chicken dance. Brad couldn't help but chuckle. They were adorable, especially Colleen who seemed intent on holding Rory's hand and leading him around. The older adults showcased their moves and somehow managed to weave their way through the children.

"I didn't realize this event was so huge," Brad remarked.

"Yeah. Even the mayor made an appearance for some fish."

"I must have missed him."

Sean sipped his beer. "My dad have you on the fryer?"

Brad made a face. "You know it."

Sean gestured. "Well, you're free now. Eat up."

Brad forked some of the green beans into his mouth. Sat up a little as the taste exploded on his tongue. He cut a bite of cod, dipped it in the delicious, homemade tartar sauce. "I can see why this place is hopping," he said. "This is really good food."

"Yeah. We like it homemade and traditional here. Some of the parishes hold Mexican-themed fish fries—like fish tacos and quesadillas. Some toss in other entrees. We just stick to cod and catfish."

"Why mess with a good thing?" Brad agreed as he continued to eat. The crowd had thinned somewhat, but most had remained to socialize and listen to the band. His gaze tracked back to where Scarlett sat at the dessert table.

She'd unwrapped a piece of cake and as she took a bite, her mouth wrapped around the tines of the fork. His libido gave a little leap.

"She's something, isn't she?" Sean said.

Caught staring, Brad turned. "Who?"

"My sister," Sean clarified.

Time to be a straight shooter. "Yeah, she is."

"I'm glad you managed to get her back here. So are my parents."

"I only provided a place to stay," Brad said. He took a few more bites. "That's all I did."

"Well, my mom tried for two years. How'd you manage it?"

"It was just a combination of things. Lucky timing, maybe."

"We're really glad to have her back. We were worried about her."

Brad nodded. "I'm glad I was able to help. Todd told me he'd like to see her be near her family if anything ever happened to him."

"Did you guys talk about that a lot?"

Brad shrugged. Hedged. "Not really. No guy wants to contemplate his mortality."

"True. Well, thanks, man."

Praise always made Brad uncomfortable. "Really, it's nothing. I told him that I'd look after her. That's all." Using his fork, he pointed to his plate. "This is good potato salad. I swear, I'm never looking at a fish fry the same again."

"They'll make you work again next week. I get out of

157

it because Maureen's manning the cash drawer and someone has to watch the kids."

"Starting March sixth, I'm working three Fridays in a row. Just how the schedule works. So I'm not on fry duty forever."

"Lucky excuse."

Brad continued to eat. Then he felt the hairs on his neck prickle. He turned and noticed a couple of women staring at him. When they realized he'd caught them looking, they quickly glanced away. Sean noticed.

"What's with that?" he asked.

"They probably recognize me from the calendar," Brad said with a shrug. "That's usually what it is. I'm used to it."

"They're looking at you again."

Brad swiveled and gave the women a smile. One of them blushed. Then Brad let his gaze trail back over to Scarlett and frowned. She wasn't alone. Tommy had engrossed her in animated conversation. Brad's green-eyed monster began to stir.

"That's Tommy," Sean said. "He's a friend of mine. She's known him forever. You look a little peaked. You're not jealous, are you?"

"Of course not," Brad lied. "We ran into him at the ball last weekend. He said he'd be here." Brad chewed slowly. Observed. Tightened his fingers on his silverware as Tommy leaned over the dessert table. Squeezed harder on his poor knife as whatever Tommy said made Scarlett laugh.

Brad wanted to make her laugh like that. Wanted to

give her moments of pure happiness and joy—those moments of contentment that had nothing to do with desire or lust, but the kind that would keep you warm when you were old and gray.

"He's a widower."

"He told us."

Sean cocked his head. "You didn't like him?"

Brad gave an exaggerated shrug. "He seems like a nice guy. I don't know him."

He didn't like this conversation. Didn't like the fact that Tommy still stood at the dessert table, chatting up Scarlett. Shouldn't he go find his own child?

"So are you sure Todd didn't have any other thoughts about Scarlett?"

The question caught Brad off guard. His head snapped back to Sean. Eyes narrowed. "What do you mean?"

"You just said Todd told you that he hoped Scarlett came back to St. Louis. Did he tell you anything else?"

The cod Brad was eating went down wrong. He coughed, grabbed his cola and took a long drink. "You okay?" Sean asked. "Sorry if that came out of the blue. I mean, I know we don't like to contemplate our mortality, but Maureen and I had to name guardians for our kids. Got me to thinking. If something happened to me, I wouldn't want her to be alone the rest of her life, you know?"

Brad drained his cola in a buy for time. Oh, hell. He needed an ally. Might as well. "We went out for beers one night once he reenlisted." Brad paused. Scarlett remained in animated conversation with Tommy. "When you do what we do, you pretend you're not going to die. You know there's a high probability you might, but you ignore it. It's the elephant in the room. Even as a first responder, there's always that risk. Hell, there's a risk every day, I guess."

He shook the plastic cup. Rattled the ice. Wished he'd opted for beer. Wondered how rude it would be if he got up to get a cold one. He'd get Sean another too.

"Todd didn't want her to be alone all her life. No man would. He'd want his beloved to be happy. Not miserable. Not alone." Brad chewed some ice.

Sean nodded. "Tommy went through loss. He and Scarlett have that in common."

"They do," Brad agreed, more and more unsettled the longer Scarlett talked. Jealousy sucked. After all, what did he and Scarlett really have in common besides some lust? She'd chosen Todd before Brad had even had a chance. He didn't want the same thing to happen again.

"I know he's looking," Sean said.

Brad's fingers tightened on the clear plastic cup. He was floundering in what was new dating territory. He'd screwed it up as recently as this morning. In a competition, Tommy would win hands-down.

At that moment, Scarlett must have sensed something, for she swiveled her head so she could see around Tommy. "What?" she mouthed at her brother and Brad.

But before Brad could try to answer, a shadow fell across him. "Hi. Are you Brad Silverman?"

He glanced up. One of the two women from earlier stood next to him, the other behind her. She stared at him intently. "You're the one in the calendar, right? Mr. July?" A diamond engagement ring glittered on her ring finger. "Can I have your autograph?"

"Uh, sure," Brad said. He took the paper and pen she thrust at him. "Your name?"

"Sybil. Would you do one for my friend Kathy as well?"

"Of course," Brad said, writing, *To Sybil, best wishes. Brad Silverman.* For Kathy he wrote, *To Kathy, all the best. Brad Silverman.*

"Thanks so much." Sybil held out her phone. "How about a picture?"

Brad hated selfies, but as they surrounded him, he smiled as he had thousands of times before. She reviewed it. "Perfect. Will you be at the auction?"

Brad saw Karen wasn't wearing a ring. She gave him a smile, but it didn't make him react like Scarlett's. "Should be a lot of fun. Lots of silent auction items and a great chance to help pick the next calendar guys. I have to go but I am not up for sale."

"Too bad. But we'll see you there," Sybil said. She was clearly the pair's leader. "Thanks so much." She fingered her autographed paper and waved it as she and Karen moved off.

"Wow," Sean said, clearly impressed.

"Yeah," Brad said with far less enthusiasm. "I'll be up on someone's Instagram again."

"So what was that all about?" Scarlett approached and Brad's heart jumped.

"They asked for Brad's autograph," Sean told her. "That calendar must be a bonanza for you in the ladies department."

Brad shrugged noncommittally. If he told the truth—that all the attention was actually creepy—Sean wouldn't believe him anyway. In the month following the calendar's debut, women had stopped by the firehouse nonstop. The other calendar models had complained as well—and this was St. Louis, where you could sit in a restaurant next to a professional baseball or football player and not one person would approach the table until after they were finished with their meal, if then.

But for some reason, those protocols didn't seem to apply. He'd been ogled. Had drinks sent his way. Posed for selfies. Been the recipient of letters, e-mails and phone numbers. Two months into the year and the attention was waning a little—thank goodness—but he'd still be gracing people's walls in July. Hopefully by then all the fuss would be over. The new guys would be getting their photos done in June, and before that there was the auction. Hopefully that would take the attention off. Make him old news.

"Saw you talking to Tommy," Sean told his sister. "He's a nice guy."

"We ran into each other at the ball. We're talking about getting our kids together." She tucked a loose strand of hair behind her ear. "Haven't decided when or where."

Brad had made a career of studying conflict situations.

She wasn't lying. She wasn't evading. She literally meant that they hadn't made plans. Raw relief filled him, for he hated the idea of her dating Tommy. However, at the same time, his rational side knew Scarlett wasn't a possession. Even if Brad and Scarlett became an item, she could have male friends. Even go do things with them.

Todd's number one hope had been that she find someone. Brad just wanted it to be him.

And all he and Scarlett had shared were a few kisses. Lust, he'd told her. "I think it's a great idea," he said.

"You do?" Scarlett quickly masked her shock. Frowned at him.

"Yeah. Why not? Can't a girl have guy friends? You do want to have playdates for Colleen. It's not like you're planning on dating him. Do you want to date him?"

"He is looking," Sean added helpfully, oblivious to the raw undercurrent or the intense way Brad held her gaze. "He's a great guy."

Tommy had moved up on praise from "good" earlier. Scarlett caught the sales pitch and responded testily, "I haven't even been in town a month and you're already trying to fix me up."

Brad held up his hands. Made a stop motion. "Don't throw this back on me. I said friends. There is nothing wrong with guys and girls being friends."

"Like us?" Scarlett arched a brow. He knew she was thinking of their kiss. Sean's eyes darted back and forth between the two.

"I would hope after all we've been through that we're

163

already friends." Brad really wished he'd gotten that beer.

Colleen raced up, a welcome diversion before the conversation went further downhill. "Mommy, I want more cake. Can I have more cake, Mommy?"

"May I," Scarlett corrected, distracted. "Is Granny still over at the cake table?"

Pigtails bounced as Colleen shook her head. "No. She's gone and I'm not allowed in the kitchen. She told me."

"No, you're not, so I'll come with you." She took Colleen's hand and walked away.

"What was all that about?" Sean asked.

"What?" Brad stood. Lifted his plate so he could take it to the busser station.

"All this friend talk."

"I believe it means Scarlett is in control of her future and doesn't want us meddling in her choices."

Sean rose, and grabbed his own place setting. "She is stubborn. Won't see what's right in front of her unless it hit her in the face. I only want her happy."

"We all do, but she has to figure out what makes her happy on her own." Brad crossed the room and placed his plate and silverware on the metal shelf that led into the kitchen's wash area. He tossed the empty plastic cup into a waste bin. Glanced around. Scarlett had settled Colleen down at a nearby table with a small piece of cake. He approached them. "I'm headed home. Looks like things are wrapping up anyway."

"The band has another song and then people will start

to clean up," she confirmed. Expectant green eyes looked up at him. "Will I see you later?"

"Working in the morning. Want to get some sleep tonight."

"Oh." She seemed disappointed.

"I'm off Sunday. Let's catch up then. I want your advice on some house projects." He really didn't, but he had no idea what else to say and he wanted to see her. Around Scarlett he felt as awkward as a sixth-grade boy with his first crush. He leaned over, kissed her cheek, headed to retrieve his coat.

Scarlett watched him leave. He had a commanding figure. Great backside. She waited, hopefully, but he never glanced back once, so she shook herself, broke the endless stare. Colleen had eaten all her cake. "Go put the plate on the counter," she told her daughter, tracking her movements as she approached the opening in the wall.

"Scarlett? Hey!" A tall brunette held a sleeping one-year-old boy in her arms. "You and I need to still make more plans!"

The cloud of doom vanished. "Jenni! I've been meaning to call you. Or send you a message. I've been so busy. A terrible person. I'm sorry I didn't do it earlier."

"I assumed your life was still crazy. Figured if I hadn't heard from you by the end of next week that I'd hunt you down. Was that Brad Silverman who just left?"

"He's my landlord." Scarlett realized she kept saying that, but really, what else was he?

"You're going to have to tell me how you managed

that. If I weren't happily married . . ."

"It's nothing like that," Scarlett said, coloring. "He was best man at my wedding."

"Well, I wouldn't let that stop me. Here comes my husband. Call me tomorrow, okay? Do not forget."

"I won't," Scarlett promised, watching them leave.

"Look at you," her mom gushed, coming up. "Now aren't you glad you came? You've already reconnected with a lot of people. See, I knew moving home would be good for you."

"So you said," Scarlett mumbled.

"I saw you talking to Tommy Rourke. He's a good catch."

"Mom!" Scarlett protested.

But Bernadette had no shame. She charged full-speed ahead. "What? He is. He's a day trader. Works from home so he can stay home with his son. Isn't that awesome? He also has two employees. Makes megabucks. Has an in-ground pool. Colleen would love to play in that."

"Who?" Maureen asked. She and Sean had rounded up their kids and joined the group.

"Tommy Rourke," Scarlett's mom said.

"He and Scarlett plan on doing a playdate," Sean filled in. Scarlett shot death rays at her brother but he failed to keep his mouth shut. "They haven't set a date yet."

"Oh, that's lovely." With glee, Scarlett's mom clasped her hands together. "He lives in one of those mansions on Hawthorne. You and Colleen can walk over it's so close."

"How nice," Scarlett replied, irritation growing. The

man who made her weak at the knees had walked out without a backward glance. The one who didn't owned a mansion but did own a house she loved. "Stop picking out china. It's a playdate. Nothing more."

"It's a gorgeous house," Maureen gushed. "Totally redone. Huge yard. Rory plays with Kyle. The attic is this huge room with bay windows and . . ." She stopped, stricken. "Sorry. Makes Sean think I don't appreciate what we have when I go on like this." She gave him a quick kiss.

"I like Kyle's house," Rory said. He'd been silently listening. "We can ride our trikes inside."

"The third floor is one huge open playroom," Sean said. "Indoor climbing things, a place for tricycles. Well, you'll see it, I'm sure."

"Brad's building me a playroom." Colleen, not to be left out, inserted herself into the conversation. "It's pink. I like our house."

"I do too," Scarlett said, deciding to get moving before her daughter began talking about how her mommy and Brad had "spilled" paint. "Let's go get your coat. It's time to go."

"Can we come here again?"

"Of course."

The drive home took fewer than five minutes and Scarlett pulled into the recently cleared space next to Brad's SUV. She could see a faint glow of lights coming from the studio apartment windows. Her phone beeped, but she ignored the device in favor of getting Colleen ready for bed. She followed suit, and it wasn't until she climbed into bed herself that she checked her text messages. As it had beeped when she went by the garage, she assumed it was from Brad. Instead, the number was foreign. *Great seeing you. You are in my phone. Get me in yours too and I can't wait to see you again. Jenni.*

Scarlett pushed aside her disappointment. What was that about the one you wanted wasn't the one who wanted you? Brad wanted to get to know her, yet he'd walked away. She leaned back against her bed, lifted the book she'd been reading and set it back down. She thought of Jenni and the warm welcome. She had to concentrate on those things, she told herself. Making friends was what was important.

As for Brad, what was that saying about men? That the answer to what they really were thinking was nothing? That women spend hours analyzing every minute detail and nuance of a situation and the guy in question hadn't even given what happened a second thought? Yeah, that sounded about right. She probably wasn't on his mind like he was on hers.

Then there was Tommy. He'd given her his business card. Made it very clear they should get their kids together. His interest had been clear—he'd hoped they'd get together too, sans kids, for a movie or a play. But Tommy didn't make her heart race the way Brad did. Still, she'd be a fool to not at least follow up and see if they were compatible. Houses on Hawthorne started at half a million, and that was an as-is property in need of renovation. He seemed like a stable, stay-at-home guy with a profitable business. The complete opposite of Todd. If nothing else, they could just be friends.

Heck, she wasn't going to kiss every man she met.z

She sent Jenni a text back with a *Me too.*

Then she took a deep breath. Found the business card and sent a text to Tommy with one line. *This is my number. Scarlett.*

She experienced an odd mixture of adrenaline and anticipation. This was it, the next step. She stared at her phone for a moment. The text read delivered. Then she put her phone on silent, turned it over on the nightstand and turned out the light.

***

Frustrated with his behavior, Brad had known he wouldn't get any sleep without working off some steam. While he'd still craved that beer, he'd avoided pulling a bottle out of the refrigerator. Back when Todd had first died, Brad drank a little too much. He'd let that precarious control he always held slip away. While he'd not crossed into needing twelve steps, he'd reined himself in. Given up women. Limited the booze.

He hated being out of control. So he locked up his studio and went for a head-clearing walk. He'd been walking back up Victor Street when he'd seen the light in Scarlett's bedroom go out.

He stopped out in front. He remembered the first time he'd seen this house, which had been before his enlistment even ended. He'd been visiting his parents, when, while out on a run, he'd noticed a For Sale sign. He'd turned down Victor and taken a look at the hundred-year-old diamond in the rough. The front porch had been sagging. Paint had been peeling. The brick tuck-pointing had looked forlorn. Yet instinct told him that he needed to see the inside.

That had been worse. Sixties appliances. Water stains from where pipes had leaked. But as Realtors like to say, the bones were solid. As the market was in a downturn and the house had become one of those forgotten, languishing listings, he'd gotten the place for far less than the list price. Not a steal, as he'd had to gut it to make it livable, but definitely worth the investment when coupled with the historic tax credits.

So he'd bought it, solidifying his desire to leave the service. Then Todd had died, and shortly afterward Brad's time in the Navy ended. He'd moved home, begun the renovations, and gone through the fire academy and gotten a job. Rehab had kept his mind off everything. Now the house was almost done.

Low-voltage lighting lit the exterior, giving the red brick a cheery glow. The porch no longer sagged, paint no longer peeled and new mortar brightened the entire façade. What had been an endless renovation had become a home.

Scarlett's home. Brad exhaled and watched his breath form a misty cloud. He had no idea how you pursued a woman, but damn it, he wanted a serious relationship with her. He'd never wooed anyone before, but he could figure it out. Hell, he'd never wanted a woman long enough to make any kind of investment, or put in any real time, and all because he'd met the woman he knew was meant for him. And now she was inside.

So he stood there, staring at his house. He'd already made one big commitment—he'd committed to a house. He'd poured every spare minute into bringing something back from the dead.

A police car drove down the road and Brad exhaled a whoosh of breath, creating a second, small vapor cloud. One had to love Mrs. Boggiano, queen of the neighborhood watch and nosy neighbor extraordinaire.

The officer didn't put on his lights, just pulled over to the curb and opened the door. "I live here," Brad told him, taking his hands out of his pockets. "Just out for a walk. If I could get my ID?"

The officer nodded and Brad retrieved his wallet. Keeping the car between them, he tossed it onto the cruiser's hood. The officer grabbed it, flipped it open, read Brad's address. Saw his firefighter ID. Tossed it back. "Sorry," he said. "We got a call."

"Mrs. Boggiano, I'm sure. I don't think she ever sleeps. But she keeps the neighborhood safe and we all love her for it." Brad pocketed his wallet.

"I'll let her know it was nothing. So what firehouse?"

"Marine unit. Out of Station Eleven. Near Seventh and Broadway. I'm on duty tomorrow."

"Your face seems familiar. I've probably seen you around before."

Brad shoved his hands back in his pockets. "Well, I'm in that damn calendar."

The officer laughed. "Yeah, maybe that's it. My mom bought one as a gag gift for my wife."

Brad said nothing and the cop's radio crackled. "Gotta go. Take care."

"You too," Brad said. "Thanks."

"No problem. Just doing my job."

Brad knew exactly what that meant. The officer slid back into the patrol car and drove off, and Brad walked between his house and the neighbor's using the concrete path he'd added last summer. He opened the gate and moved into the backyard. The motion detector he'd installed brought the floodlight on, and he made it to his garage apartment long before it flashed off.

He stripped his clothes off. Wedged himself into the water closet. Washed his hands in the tiny sink before dropping into bed. Tried to let the weight of the world drop away as he closed his eyes.

Instead he saw Scarlett's face when he'd walked out in a towel. At first she'd stared at him in shock. Then he'd watched how her irises had darkened. She hadn't realized it, but her nipples had pebbled. His body had hardened even though he'd worked out some sexual frustration in the shower. Not that it had helped. Thinking about her right now was making him hard. But he couldn't do casual sex. Not with Scarlett. He wanted to be with her long term. Saw their budding relationship like he had the house—a big commitment he was willing to make. He had to go all-in, and if he failed, learn to live with nothing.

He just prayed he wouldn't fail.

Chapter Eight

Brad's firehouse was a modern, three-bay structure that faced South Seventh. Running on battery, Scarlett's Prius made no sound as she found the parking lot off Shenandoah and pulled in. "Are we here?" Colleen asked from her car seat.

"Yes." Scarlett's nerves tingled as she pressed the power button.

"Do you think Brad will like our cookies?"

"I'm sure he'll love them. He suggested we bring them, didn't he?" The latter part was more to calm her nerves than for Colleen to answer. Earlier that morning, Brad had texted her and asked what she was doing. She'd told him she and Colleen were baking sugar cookies, and he'd asked them if there were extras. She'd said yes, and he'd suggested she bring them to the firehouse.

"Will I get to see the fire truck?"

"I'm sure you will. You may unclip."

Scarlett came around and let Colleen out of the car. She reached inside and removed the Tupperware container full of cookies. Brad must have been watching for them, for he opened the door when they arrived, and led them inside.

"We brought you cookies. I put the sprinkles on myself," Colleen told him proudly.

"I can't wait to try one. I bet they're delicious. Come on in. Meet my crew."

He led them into the bay, where a few guys stood around polishing the truck. "Scarlett, this is the crew I work with. Lewis, Roger and my lieutenant, Chris. She brought us cookies."

"Nice to meet you," the men chorused, and Scarlett peeled back the lid and held them out.

"Oh, those look good," Chris said. He reached for one, took it out and popped it in his mouth. "Mmm. Delicious."

That seemed to be the go sign, for the other three men also reached for cookies. "These are great," Lewis complimented.

"Thanks." Scarlett felt some of the tension ease. She'd been nervous coming here to Brad's work and meeting the guys. None of them had been at the Mayor's Ball. Yet pretty soon everyone was munching cookies, including a few guys from other crews. The container of several dozen emptied fast, and afterward, Lewis, who was older than Brad by over a decade, told Colleen she was about his granddaughter's age and lifted her into the driver's seat.

Scarlett used her phone to take a picture, and then she and Brad stepped aside as Lewis began to show Colleen the rest of the truck and Chris and Kyle inspected some equipment. "We're not bothering you, are we?"

"No, you could never be a bother. We had some cleaning and the morning's been slow. The guys saw me texting you and I told them I'd get some cookies. This way you could meet them. See where I worked. And they'll think you're awesome since you brought treats."

"So that's all it takes? Baked goods?"

His grin warmed her insides. "What can I say? We're easy." Brad placed his hand on her back and guided her a few more steps away from the truck. He wore a long-sleeve blue T-shirt with the fire department logo and blue work pants. Turnout gear was scattered around in strategic places, ready for when a call came through.

"How about we spend some time together tomorrow?" Brad asked. "I went for a walk last night to clear my head and have a few things I'd like to share. I'd rather do them face-to-face. And maybe we can do dinner. A movie. Something like that? Or something else?"

"Sure."

He smiled. Touched her arm. "Good. I'd like that. And it'll give me something to look forward to."

A loud buzzer sounded, and Scarlett jumped. Brad froze. Listened as the speaker blared out the call details. "I have to go. I'll text you later," he said.

Across the way, Lewis helped Colleen out of the quint truck. She ran over. "Mommy, what's that noise?"

"We have a call, pumpkin," Brad told her. "We have to go help some people. You'll be safe over there while we pull out." He gave Scarlett a quick kiss on her cheek, jogged over to his gear and suited up. She moved Colleen over to the spot he'd indicated and they watched as Brad pulled on his bunker pants and drew on his coat. He then climbed into the driver's seat, gave a quick wave before he pulled out, siren blaring. The other quint truck followed suit, and in the middle of the bay, the empty Tupperware sat as a lonely reminder that they'd all been eating cookies only moments before. An eerie silence fell.

"Time to go home," Scarlett said. She went and retrieved her container. Reached for Colleen's hand.

"When will Brad get back?"

"I don't know. He has to go help people."

"Is he a hero? Grandma says people who help others are heroes."

"He's a hero," Scarlett said.

Colleen nodded. "Our hero."

"Yes," Scarlett said, bundling up Colleen's coat and guiding her to the door. "That's exactly what he is."

***

"So that's your girl," Lewis said over the headphones as they rode to the scene of a two-alarm fire.

"She's my tenant," Brad shot back.

"Uh-huh," Kyle replied. "When have you ever invited a woman to the firehouse? And don't count those crazy calendar stalkers either."

"Never," Chris filled in the correct answer.

Luckily they'd reached the scene of the blaze, which meant work began and idle chatter ceased. The fire took a while to put out. But there was no rest for the weary. By midafternoon, everything changed. The calls came in one after another. Another cold front arrived, shooing away the calm weather and instead blanketing the area with freezing rain, making for slick, icy roads and lots of people playing bumper cars. They'd put out two space-heater fires, luckily minor and caught in time. Now they'd finished putting out a one-alarm fire at a local greasy spoon, which would be closed for quite a while after flames had gone up the back kitchen wall.

"Man, I could use more of those cookies your lady brought," Lewis said as they began to stow their equipment. "I'm hungry. I hope there's some grub when we get back."

"Me too." Brad slid the last of the equipment away. Around him, other crews began to load up their gear and head back to their respective houses. A news reporter stood as close to the building as allowed, waiting for the on-air light. It came on, and she began speaking. Brad hoped he wasn't on camera. He hated that.

As he took a step, he froze, his foot in midair. Was that a plaintive, tiny meow? "Guys? Do you hear that?"

"I see it. Stay still. I got it." Lewis swept in and scooped up the tiny kitten that had crawled close to the truck. The little cat was all black, except for an orange slash mark down its forehead. "Hey there," he said. "You got good instincts."

"He's lucky I saw him," Brad said, making sure nothing else was underfoot.

Lewis cradled the cat to his chest. "I'm not talking about you, I mean the cat's got good instincts. He knows his meal ticket is closed. Looks about three or four months old." The ragged thing gave the most pathetic meow ever. "The jury is still out on your instincts, especially if you don't think the cookie lady is anything but your tenant."

"Ha-ha," Brad drolled.

"Does it need oxygen?" Roger asked. The truck carried pet oxygen masks.

Lewis gave it a once-over. "I don't think he was in the smoke. Think he was outside."

"Well, what do we do with it? We can't keep it at the firehouse," Chris said. He was the man in charge. "Where can it go? I don't want to leave it here."

Tucked into Lew's arms, the cat was already purring.

"It's clearly a stray. We can't leave it here," Roger agreed with Chris. He looked at Lewis. "Your wife's the crazy cat lady always rescuing something or another. What do you suggest?"

"We can't leave it here, but I can't take it. I've got four already," Lewis said. The kitten in his arms gave a small sigh and closed its eyes, safe and secure. "And my wife will kill me if we turn it in to the shelter, even a no-kill one. Most of those are full. You all know how Peggy is."

"Oh yeah," Roger agreed with a sage nod. "No one

wants to cross Peggy."

"You know," Lew said thoughtfully, "your tenant's little girl was telling me how much she wanted a kitten."

They all turned as one to look at Brad. A pit formed in his stomach. He blinked. "Uh, no, she didn't."

"Uh, yeah, she did," Lew added. "I asked her if she had pets and she said no. Asked me if I had some. Told her I had cats. Then she told me her mom had promised her one."

Brad couldn't tell if Lew was lying or not. Knew it didn't matter.

Chris grinned. "Don't you have that huge house?"

"I'm in the studio over the garage while I fix it up. Remember?"

"Plenty of space," Lew said. "And how can you resist this face?"

Lew turned, and all Brad could see was the sweet face of a sleepy, tiny kitten. It gave another tiny meow and snuggled closer.

"Hey, did you rescue that kitten from the fire?" The reporter had come over to the truck. She gestured, and the cameraman began rolling. "I'm outside Essie's where firefighters have just rescued a kitten caught up in the event. Can you tell us what will happen to it?"

Used to the press, Chris stepped forward. "It appears to be a stray and not to have suffered any injuries. Brad here is going to take it home."

The reporter swung toward him, her eyes wide as she recognized him. "You're Brad Silverman. So Mr. July is going to provide a home for an orphaned kitten."

"Yes," Brad replied. Lewis was already climbing into the truck with it. Brad turned, headed for the truck.

"Well, viewers, that's a happy ending to this terrible event," he heard her say as she recorded more story.

Brad slid into his seat and buckled up. That was the thing about being the newest member of the crew. You were always outranked, and these guys had worked together for about three years before Brad had come along. He pulled on his headset.

"I'll text Peggy and ask her to bring some food and litter," Lewis offered via headset.

"That will work," Chris confirmed. "Cheer up, Brad. Sometimes it's destiny. Now let's get out of here."

Yeah, right. Destiny. Which was why Brad found himself walking up to Scarlett's back door at eight thirty Sunday morning, a cat carrier in one hand and a seven-pound bag of food in the other. The rest of the cat's stuff was in his SUV. Who knew cats needed so much gear? He rang the bell with his elbow, then set stuff down and used his key. The darn cat was howling up a storm inside the cat carrier, and he couldn't blame him. He knew what it was like to feel trapped.

He entered the kitchen. Heard little feet running down the stairs as Colleen flew into the kitchen before her mother. She saw the carrier immediately. "Kitty!" she shrieked. The cat scooted to the back of the carrier.

"Shh," he told her, setting it on the island. Her hands were already up in the air reaching, and he lifted her onto the bar chair. "Don't scare it. He's had a rough night." Brad didn't add that the beast had cried most of the night, keeping him awake when he did find a few minutes for sleep between calls. He'd finally taken the animal out of the carrier and let it sleep on his chest, for that had been the only way the kitten had settled. He had to admit, he'd grown a bit attached, especially after the cat had started purring in his arms after a feeding. The little guy had needed saving, and so Brad stepped up to the plate. He simply hadn't expected the emotions that came with. No way was he letting him live elsewhere now.

"If kitty is going to live here, you have to learn some rules."

Green eyes so like Scarlett's watched him intently. "Okay."

"First, you have to talk softly to the kitty. And when I take him out, you have to be very gentle."

Colleen hadn't stopped nodding. "I will. I can be very gentle."

Brad opened the cage and took out the frightened animal. Sensing he was in Brad's arms, the kitty calmed. Brad leaned over and let Colleen pet it, and then he transferred the animal to Colleen's arms. "Shh," she told the kitty. She cradled it like a doll and scratched behind its ears. The cat settled down immediately and began purring. "Does it have a name? Do I get to name the kitty? This is my kitty, right?"

"Right."

"What are you two talking about?" Scarlett came into

the kitchen. She'd swiped her hair into a ponytail and wore a baby-blue T-shirt and blue striped pajama pants. She wiped her eyes. "Sorry, my alarm just went off. Why did you ring the bell?" Then her eyes widened. Saw what Colleen held. "What is that?"

"Look, Mommy, Brad brought me a kitty." Colleen began rocking the cat. "He's purring, Mommy. Listen." She lifted her arms up so her mom could hear.

"Found it after a call," Brad said. "If you don't believe me, it made the late news."

"You were on the news?"

"Essie's had a grease fire. Then we found the kitten. Reporter made it even a bigger deal than it was."

Scarlett was dumbfounded. "It probably has fleas."

"Nope. Got flea dipped last night. Ear mite treatment too. Lewis's wife, Peggy, came by the station and treated it. Brought all sorts of cat things that we'd need and gave me a detailed shopping list for the rest."

"She's always wanted a cat." Scarlett's hands went to her hips. Her chin jutted forward. "But I thought we'd wait a while. You could have discussed this with me first."

Brad knew she wanted to kill him. "Is she allergic?"

"No."

"Then the kitten comes with the house," he said easily. "You already have the landlord's approval, so no worries there. I'll pay the vet bills. I mean, I can't give him up now that everyone in the city thinks I've rescued him, and he'll be happier over here with you than out above the garage. Peggy says it'll need shots and fixing. It's a boy."

Colleen's happiness was infectious. "Mommy, he has a Harry Potter mark. I'm calling him Harry. Cute Harry," Colleen cooed. "Do you like it when I scratch your ears, Harry?" Harry responded with a mewling noise and a purr.

She moved closer, trying to share Colleen's excitement. "So this is Harry Harrison?" Scarlett asked, adding their last name.

"No, Mommy. This is Harry Potter." She may not have yet seen the movies, but Colleen knew who Harry Potter was. "He's my kitty."

Scarlett knew when she was beaten. No way would she ask Colleen to give up cute little Harry, and besides, he was adorable. She reached out and scratched the top of his tiny head.

"Peggy says if we keep him inside, he'll never want to go outside. Then we don't need to worry about losing him. But we should get him microchipped anyway."

"Can he sleep with me?" Colleen asked.

"Yes," Brad inserted before Scarlett could check that.

"Can he sit on the couch?"

Scarlett gave a resigned sigh. "I'm sure he's going to be all over the house. Although we'll need to train him to stay off the counters."

"I've got a litter box out in the car and litter. Peggy recommends giving him limited range until he gets used to his new surroundings. She suggested putting the litter box in the bathroom so that way the kitten can have free rein between your and Colleen's bedrooms for a few days. She says we'll know when he's ready to broaden his horizons and then we can give him the run of the house."

"I see you have everything all figured out," Scarlett said, watching as Colleen was already taking the kitten back upstairs. "I am so not happy with you."

Brad grinned. "You weren't before."

"True, but you blindsided me with a kitten."

"And you've already fallen in love with it. Admit it."

She sighed. "Fine. But couldn't you have called? A head's-up would have been nice."

"Sorry. We went on call after call and by the time I got back and Peggy'd taken care of him, I figured it was too late. Oh, Peggy gave me the name of her vet. We met her at the Mayor's Ball. Kat Saunders."

"You do realize that had we adopted a pet from the shelter it wouldn't have been as much money as this free cat is going to cost."

He shrugged. Gave her another endearing grin. "No big deal. Little guy's worth it and I told you I'd handle it."

"I've got money," Scarlett said.

"I know, but I brought it home. I'm working again tomorrow, but I can call and make an appointment."

"I'll do it. And you better go outside and get those cat supplies. Any accidents and you're cleaning them."

"Yes, ma'am." Brad gave her a grin and a salute and went back out the door. A few minutes later he returned carrying a covered litter box and a thirty-five-pound yellow plastic tub of litter. "There's more," he told her, setting it down.

"More?"

"Yeah. Peggy gave us a scratching post and a bunch of cat toys. She and Lewis foster cats and have four of their own. The carrier is the only thing we'll need to return."

"That's sweet of them. This is a lot of stuff."

"Yeah," he said, heading back out the door. "She says we will need a cat tower too. We have plenty of space for one."

"Great," Scarlett called after him. Now they were pet owners. She grabbed the litter box and hoisted the tub of litter. Used to lifting her daughter, it weighed nothing. She carried both upstairs to the en suite bathroom. Found a spot for the litter box in an out-of-the-way corner. Realized they'd need to keep a broom upstairs so that they could sweep up any loose litter that the kitten tracked onto the floor. And they'd need a supply of small trash bags in order to keep the box clean.

Brad came upstairs carrying a litter scoop, cat carrier and a thirty-inch carpeted scratching post. "Here you go."

"Thanks," Scarlett said, wondering where the heck she was going to put all that. "Put the carrier in the spare bedroom until we buy one. The post, oh, I don't know."

"Mommy, the kitty is climbing my curtains," Colleen called. "He's almost at the top. Harry! Come down!"

"Scratching post goes to Colleen's room," she and Brad said almost in unison. They both started laughing, and Brad lifted the carpet-covered pole and set it in the center of her room. Harry jumped down and found his scratching post. He perched atop like a giant bird, all four paws on the four-inch rounded top. He opened his mouth.

Made a plaintive meow.

"He's going to run this house," Scarlett said, stating the inevitable.

"Yeah, but she's happy," Brad pointed out. Colleen was already teasing Harry with a string. He batted at it. "How about we go to the pet store later and buy some toys?"

"Let me text my mom and tell her we're not going to make it to church," Scarlett said. "Have you eaten?"

"No."

She led him out of Colleen's room. "I'll cook something. I've got some sausage links and bacon. I'll do that instead of toast and oatmeal. Maybe some eggs."

"That's a feast."

"One you don't deserve." She paused at the top of the stairs. "You realize you've saddled us with a twenty-year commitment."

"They live that long? Hmm, the guys didn't tell me that."

"I'm sure there's a reason they conveniently forgot that fact." She began to walk down the stairs.

"Well, he'll grow up with her," Brad called after her. "I never had a pet. I would have liked one growing up."

"Seriously?" She paused. "That's sad. We had cats growing up."

"No, I was deprived. If you ever don't want him, I'll make sure he has a home with me."

"Thanks. Harry's staying with us. Colleen's been patient. Her friends had animals and she'd beg and beg."

"Then maybe it's fate. He literally walked up to us and started meowing. Most pathetic thing you'd ever seen. Do you see how skinny he is?"

"Just don't bring any more home," she warned, turning back to face him. She jabbed a finger into his chest as he stepped off the last stair. "You may be scared of your lieutenant, but I met him. He's got nothing on me. Got that?"

He captured her hand. Held it in his. "Yes, ma'am. Orders received and understood."

He let her hand go and followed her into the kitchen. Watched as she opened the refrigerator. "Here," she called.

She removed a carton of eggs and held out the container. He took it and set the eggs on the counter. She pulled open the meat drawer and removed the sausage and bacon. Handed them to him. He set those next to the eggs.

"Get the bread out of the pantry while I find the frying pan."

"Yes, ma'am."

"Cut that out or I'll hit you with this frying pan."

He opened the double doors. Poked his head around so he could see her. "Violent this morning, aren't you?"

Her hand dangled a cast-iron skillet. "You dive-bombed me with a kitten."

"Dive-bombed? What am I, a seagull?"

"You know what I mean."

He found the sliced bread. Shut the pantry and brought it over. "He'll kill any mice too."

"Mice?" She gave a small squeak.

He took the frying pan from her fingers and set it on

the counter. "I've never seen any, or signs of any. But with these old houses, you never know."

"Great. Thanks for that." She took out a bowl. Cracked a few eggs and began to whip them together. Added salt and pepper. "Grab the milk, will you?"

He complied and she added some milk and whipped it into the egg mixture. She found another frying pan, put it on the stove and turned on the gas flame. She added the sausage and it began to sizzle.

Brad took a seat at the island and watched her work. She was a machine—bacon went into the microwave to cook. Bread went into the toaster. Popped up golden brown. Eggs poured into the other skillet turned into scrambled eggs. There was something homey about watching someone you liked cook. An intimacy to the act that didn't have him wanting to run for the hills. She waved a spatula at him. "Make yourself useful and get plates out," she told him, taking the eggs off the stove.

"Sure." He jumped up. Did as directed. Got everything ready. "This is nice. Thanks for cooking."

"You're welcome. Least I can do, with you providing me this great kitchen. Did I tell you I've registered for college? I've got about a semester and a half left. I'm going back in August once Colleen goes to preschool. It's time."

"That's fantastic." He was happy for her. "I think that's a great idea."

"I've put my life on hold long enough, you know? I can finish school, get a job and still be a mom, right?"

"Right." He didn't see why not.

"I'm going to go get Colleen. Serve yourself some food."

"I'll wait."

A few minutes later the three of them sat at the island eating breakfast, with Colleen telling them all about Harry the kitten's antics. "He was sleeping when I left," she told them matter-of-factly. "He's a good kitty."

"Well, he'll have to go to the vet soon," her mom said. "I'm going to make an appointment. He has to be fixed."

"Fixed?" Colleen asked.

"That means he can't be a daddy cat," her mom said.

"Why not?"

"Because there are too many kittens in the world already that don't have homes," Scarlett said. "So Harry doesn't need to get any girl kitty pregnant. It won't hurt him and he'll be home right away."

"Okay," Colleen said. Brad marveled at the easy way kids simply accepted things. Breakfast continued easily, with Colleen asking if she could be excused once she'd finished her food.

"Wash your hands," her mom told her. "We'll have to go to the pet store later."

"I will," Colleen promised and headed back upstairs.

"She's a good kid," Brad observed.

"She is."

"Todd was a fool." The words slid out and Brad smacked his hand across his mouth. "Sorry."

"No, I often feel that way myself."

"He could have had all this." Brad gestured around the kitchen. "Should have had all this."

"Believe me, I know," Scarlett said. "There are times I get so mad at him for leaving us, you know? For the first six months, I yelled and yelled. Waited until Colleen was asleep and punched a pillow and cursed him to the moon and back. But it does nothing. Nothing." She drew breath. "It's done. It's over, and I have to focus on what's ahead, not behind. I have to let it go or I'll never move forward. I can get stuck in the moment, or I can pull myself up and live my life. I'm opting for the latter. I can't wallow any longer."

He'd stagnated himself. Understood where she was coming from. "I struggle with that. I feel as if I should have done something. I tried. Talked to him. Told him not to reenlist."

She put her hand on his arm. "You can't blame yourself."

"But I do." He wanted to tell her everything but she was standing. Moving away. His arm cooled as her touch lifted.

"Don't. We can't do anything so there's no reason to rehash it. Our doing so won't bring him back. All it does is make me sad. So come on. Help me do dishes. Let's change topics. Lighten things up. Get to know each other like you want."

"Okay." They talked about this and that as he brought everything over to the counter by the sink. She scraped the dishes, ran the disposal. Her back was toward him, but suddenly he saw her tremble.

"Hey." He reached around her and turned the water off. "What's going on?"

She rubbed the back of her left hand across her left

eye. "Nothing."

He wrapped his arms around her. Cuddled her from behind. "I'm sorry. I shouldn't have brought Todd up. I'm still trying to move past it myself."

"No, it's okay. It's always going to be our reality." She started the water, picked up a plate and began to rinse. "We have to learn to live with it and move on. We can't let him come between us. I want an us. We'll have to make peace with it."

He slid his arms down hers, took her hands in his. Warm water washed over them. "I don't want to be making you sad every time I'm here."

"You don't." At this second he was sending other, more powerful feelings through her. He took the clean plate from her hand and set it into the sink. Scarlett trembled as desire shot through her. "I like when you're here."

"I like being here. But it scares me. It feels like I'm betraying him."

Brad let the admission loose, for it was hard to concentrate on keeping secrets when he was pressed up against Scarlett's backside. He wanted to keep holding her. Concentrate only on them. Luckily she couldn't look into his eyes that somehow could see into his soul, read his heart's desire.

Scarlett leaned back more. "You're not betraying him. Life goes on and I want to feel alive again. I want passion. I don't want to have died too, you know? I deserve more."

He understood that. Told her what she wanted to hear. "I want you."

Scarlett felt his breath hot in her ear, and she could feel the proof of his desire pressed into her backside.

"Touch me." She swiveled her hand and grabbed his. Moved his fingertips to her lips and kissed his wet skin. She drew his fingers into her mouth so she could suck each digit in turn. Behind her, she heard him groan. She was in the driver's seat, she knew that, so she took his right hand from her mouth and guided it to the V of her shirt. Directed said hand under the fabric to her left breast. Five fingers caressed her breast and pebbled the nipple.

His leg urged hers open, and he slid his knee in between. The water in the sink ran, providing unheeded background noise. His left hand came to her mouth and she kissed his fingertips. Then he took that hand and plunged it underneath her front waistband, finding her folds. Her head fell back against his chest and she gasped. Wanted his lips on hers. But instead, he kissed her neck. Rolled her nipple between his fingers. Used his other hand to rub slick circles into her heated wetness.

She was going to explode. She spread her legs wider, arched her back so he could slip a finger inside, then another. Her breath grew heavier and faster as an orgasm began to build. She rode his hand hard and she twisted, making him take her mouth in his. He kissed her until she shattered, the orgasm sending waves of pleasure through her. Then the aftershocks added delightful, secondary quivers until her toes slowly uncurled. He slid his hands under the running water. Turned it off. Held her close. "I needed that," she told him. She wanted to turn, but instead, her backside remained pressed to his front.

"I know." His lips kissed her neck.

"I want more."

"I know. Me too. I can't fight it." He lowered his lips. Allowed himself to kiss her. "I just don't want to hurt you," he whispered in between nibbles. "I'd never forgive myself if I hurt you."

"I won't let you," she told him, wrapping her arms around his neck.

He ran a finger down her throat and across the fabric of the breast he'd caressed.

With a boldness he hadn't known she possessed, Scarlett reached into her bra and removed her breast. It lay there exposed in her hand, surrounded by the baby-blue fabric of her shirt. When had she become the seductress? She ran her thumb over the nipple and then reached for his head. Brought it to her breast. Gave a small cry that was music to his ears as he took her into his mouth.

He sucked and licked, felt himself harden into a rock. His knees weakened. He wanted all of her. Could feel her sensitive skin tingle under his ministrations. He lifted her up and sat her on the edge of the sink. She wrapped her legs around him and he removed her other breast so he could greedily have them both. They spilled over the blue fabric, glorious mounds of snowy flesh. "You are so beautiful," he told her, taking his time going between the two as he sucked each nipple to a pebble point. This was all for her. Between his hands and mouth, he wanted her to come. Wanted to give her another earth-shattering orgasm. "Sit back. Spread your legs."

"Huh?" She complied, finding herself straddling the sink. He grabbed the water hose, turned it on full and brought it to her core. He continued to make love to her breasts as the heated jet soaked her through her pajama bottoms. Water went everywhere, but she shattered immediately in a series of cries and trembles that told him exactly how hard she'd come. Good. He wanted her satisfied. Wanted her molten. Afterward he turned off the water, dropped the hose and readjusted her shirt. He drew her into his arms and held her close.

"Holy hell," she gasped. "Where did that come from?"

"No idea," he admitted with a grin.

She flushed. "We made a mess."

His grin never wavered. "It's tile. It cleans."

"Mommy?" Colleen called down the stairs. "Harry pooped. It's smelly."

"Reality intrudes," Scarlett said, her face still crimson from the heat.

He tucked a piece of stray hair behind her ear. "I'll take care of it. You go get dry."

"I have some clean clothes in the dryer." Scarlett watched him stride off, his step not as steady as normal. Good. She wanted him hot and bothered. Wanted him unsettled. She went to the basement laundry room and stripped down. Realized as she stood there changing that he'd gotten under her skin. She wanted whatever this was—the current reality. The right now.

Wanted it a great deal.

Chapter Nine

By Wednesday afternoon, when Jenni arrived with her kids for a playdate, Scarlett was a jumble of nerves. Brad had picked up an extra shift, so he hadn't been around much. But he'd texted, and those little gestures had helped calm her. She'd never been so intimate without actual intercourse. He'd made her come. Even over the phone, he could make her want him.

"This is such a great house." Jenni took a seat on the second-floor couch. "I'm coveting that bathroom."

"I admit I didn't know bathrooms like that really existed." On the other end of the L-shaped couch, Scarlett stretched her legs out. Jenni's one-year-old napped in the Pack 'n Play portable playpen and her older children, a three-year-old boy and a four-year-old girl, were in Colleen's room playing. "That playroom upstairs is going to be fantastic. I see lots of playdates here."

Scarlett kept an ear tuned. Occasionally she would

hear a shriek come from Colleen's bedroom, but mostly it was good, calm fun. "He worked pretty hard on it. The furniture should be arriving next week."

"He's gone above and beyond. If he even sells this place, you tell me first. I'm buying it."

"Your house is beautiful too."

"I'm just greedy for more space. We're actually saving so that we can have a bigger down payment. We'll stay in the neighborhood. I'm too much of a city girl to leave. But you let me know. Hmm. I could divorce Adam and marry Brad . . ."

"Don't you dare," Scarlett admonished, knowing her friend was joking. "I've got dibs."

"I know. And I do love my hubby. Very much." Jenni snapped her fingers. "Oh well. Darn. Brad's all yours."

"Can you keep a secret?"

"Who am I going to tell? Adam? He doesn't want to know any of this. Tell me."

"He's confusing. We have great physical chemistry but I don't know what we have beyond that."

Jenni's hazel eyes turned into saucers. "You slept with him."

Scarlett shook her head quickly. Flushed. "Uh, no. Things have not gone that far. Just some kissing. A few touches." She blushed. "Some really awesome touches."

"Really."

"I've never"—Scarlett glanced around. Lowered her voice—"come like that."

"Ooh," Jenni said. "Not even with Todd?"

"No, it's different. What if it's all fire? What if it burns out?"

"You learn to fan the flames. You learn to keep it hot, like I do with Adam."

"I failed with Todd."

"He's in the past. You were young. We women get better as we get older. Trust me."

"But what if it's only good sex? I feel like he's holding back."

"With what?"

"I don't know. But it's a feeling. And it worries me. I've never been in any relationship besides Todd and I have no idea how these things work."

"My advice is to follow your own heart. Your own gut. Ask him."

Scarlett acknowledged that advice with a tilt of her head.

"What about Tommy?" Jenni asked.

"There's no chemistry there. Brad's the only man currently on my radar. I'm not comfortable with multiple men, anyway, and I want sparks this time, you know? I want the zing."

"The zing is nice," Jenni agreed. She sipped her lemonade. "You and I are going to have to go out for wine one night. We'll make Adam babysit. Besides, Colleen's great with Brenna and AJ. We can make a night of it. What are you doing this Saturday?"

"It's the calendar auction. We're going."

Jenni snapped her fingers again, this time because she

had an idea. "Let me take Colleen for the night. She'll sleep at my house and that way your mom won't act as a chaperone. You won't have anyone to interrupt you, if you get what I mean?"

"He does walk my mom out to her car to make sure she's safe."

Jenni nodded. "Exactly. You need to seduce the pants off the sexy Mr. Silverman. See if there are some really fantastic sparks. Any extreme zing. If not, call it a day and go back to being only good friends. If that's the case, he'll make a good T man."

"T man?" She'd never heard that expression.

"Transition. Your in-between. The one who helps you breach the gap between the love of your life and whoever comes along after. You've never dated. So play around. Enjoy yourself. Just be sure to set the ground rules first."

"I don't know what those are. And I'm not sure I know how to play around."

Jenni smiled. "Trust me. You'll figure it out."

***

The Sexy Public Servants of St. Louis bachelor auction and calendar audition was a semiformal event held in a local hotel ballroom. Most women were dressed in club clothing, which meant lot of tight, short dresses. The men dragged along wore oxford shirts and jeans. The only ones wearing suits were the men participating in the bachelor auction as they vied for a spot in the next calendar.

Brad wore one of those suits and he certainly wasn't happy about it. He'd found out he'd been added to the charity bill as bachelor number thirty fewer than twenty-four hours prior to the event, after the guy in his house had come down with the flu.

She could tell he wasn't happy—he drummed his fingers on the table when he wasn't nursing his beer. However, he looked totally handsome. He'd set off the dark blue material with a red-and-white polka-dotted tie.

"It's going to be fine," Scarlett said, reaching over to cover his hand.

"I don't want to be bought," he hissed. "I didn't sign up for this."

"But you're filling in. People will understand." Scarlett shifted, careful not to damage the little black dress, another splurge. She'd been out with Colleen pursuing the winter clothing sales and there it was, practically calling her name. She'd never worn anything quite so scandalous.

Not that the dress was inappropriate. The scooped bodice only hinted at the V of her breasts, allowing her to wear a bra. However, the fabric was stretchy and form fitting, and she'd had to keep pulling the dress down to mid-thigh. Otherwise the whole wide world would see she wore only a little black thong that was really little more than butt floss.

She was seated with the same people as at the Mayor's Ball. She'd gotten to know Dr. Kat Saunders better, for she was the vet who'd done Harry's neutering.

After dinner, Brad was called away to join the men

being auctioned. "How are things going?" Kat asked.

"Good," Scarlett said.

"Brad reminds me a little of my Jack," Kat said. "Tough on the outside but a sweetheart on the inside."

"He is that," Scarlett said.

"I hear a *but* in your voice."

"We're just taking things slowly."

"I was a little reluctant at first too," Kat confided. "Jack and I saved this dog, and we had that in common, but he also hated Christmas. Worse, we were just fake dating to keep his meddling parents off his back. We had some misunderstandings. So whatever you have going between the two of you, if you love him you'll work it out."

"Oh, I'm not . . ." Scarlett paused. Did she love Brad? He certainly occupied her thoughts. "I wish I could save him from being up there."

"So bid on him."

Scarlett shook her head. "I don't have the kind of money these women are tossing around." Bachelor number ten had gone for five thousand.

"Maybe they'll be out of money by that time."

"One can only hope," Scarlett said, as bachelor eleven went for three thousand. "I'm going to hit the restroom. Maybe hit the bar for more wine. Think I'm going to need it."

She wove her way toward the ballroom's exit doors. The path went by where the remaining men were lined up. Brad reached out and caught her arm. He pulled her to him. "Hey. You have to save me."

She blinked. "How?"

"Buy me."

"With what?"

Before Brad could answer, a white-haired lady said, "Brad, you need to queue up. Sweetie, you want him, you need to bid."

"Virginia, she's my girlfriend and I'm falling in love with her. You need to let me out of this. Or let me buy myself."

Scarlett stared at Brad, who held her close and looked into her eyes. "Really? You love me."

"Really," Brad told her. "I planned on telling you later tonight. I don't want you to think I want this date." He tightened his grip. "All I want is you."

"Oh," Scarlett said, and Brad swooped down for a quick, tender kiss. Scarlett's heart swelled. When Brad broke it off, he turned to Virginia. "I'm only here so you weren't short a firefighter. Why can't twenty-nine be enough?"

Virginia appeared peaked. "Oh, this is awkward. We'll be sure your buyer knows you're taken. Sorry. Move along."

By the time Scarlett returned to the table, bachelor twenty-six had reached the stage. Brad was the last one and he strode onto the stage with a scowl. As he passed the woman from before, she must have said something because he schooled his face into a forced smile.

"Last but not least," she said, "we have this year's Mr. July, Brad Silverman. He's a firefighter, a handyman and a jack-of-all-trades and he's subbing in for the man on your program who was too sick to be here. Bid well." She walked off the stage.

"It'll be fine," Kat said.

"He told me he loved me."

"What? Oh, not good. Do you want me to bid?"

"Who is offering five hundred?" the auctioneer said.

Fourteen paddles shot up. Scarlett glanced around the room, seeing women of all ages bidding. The bidding went in fifty-dollar increments, and as he reached a thousand, only eight women were bidding. By the time he hit twelve hundred, three more had dropped out. At thirteen hundred, only four remained bidding.

"See, the last one always goes for less. He wasn't on the program, so no one knew," Kat consoled. "I'll bid."

"I could never pay you back," Scarlett said as those four still bidding quickly pushed Brad's total up to two thousand dollars. Then three. Two women remained.

"Six thousand," a voice said. Scarlett swiveled in her seat to see Virginia, the woman from earlier, holding high the number-one paddle.

The auctioneer seemed to get her drift, because he quickly cut off the other bids and yelled, "Going once, twice, sold to number one, Virginia."

"Well, I'll be damned," Kat said.

"Who is that?" Scarlett demanded. "She heard Brad say he loved me. Why would she do this?"

"You mean you've never met the calendar committee chair?"

"No, but I will now." Scarlett stood before Kat could

say anything and rushed off toward where she'd found Brad earlier. When she reached him, Virginia was standing there. "He's all yours, dear," she said, pushing him forward. Scarlett's anger dissolved into confusion, especially when she saw the huge wedding ring on Virginia's finger.

"I don't understand. I can't pay you back," Scarlett said.

Virginia smiled. "Consider it my wedding gift. I adore true love. My Parker and I have been married fifty years."

"Really, we can't. I must insist . . ."

Scarlett began to protest, but Brad grabbed her hand. "Thank you," he said, leaning over to give Virginia a kiss on the cheek. "We appreciate this."

"I want to be invited. I'll be offended otherwise," she called after them.

Brad wrapped his arm around Scarlett and propelled her toward the doors. "I'm ready to go, aren't you?"

They stepped out into the bright hallway. The hotel coat check was across the way. "Brad, we can't let her pay for you."

He kept guiding her across the floor. "Yes, we can. She's richer than Croesus and will be insulted if we don't. And she found a solution to keeping me with you. I want to be with you, Scarlett."

"I want to be with you too," she said.

"Then let's go home." He ran his forefinger from her shoulder down her arm to her hand. She trembled and he took her fingers in his. "Do you know what you do to me? I'm serious when I say I'm going to be your guy and that I love you."

She leaned forward and put both of her hands on his forearms. "Then if you're already mine, I know what I'd like you to do to me. Please don't stop tonight. Make love to me."

They got in the car, and Brad leaned across the center console to give her a kiss to end all kisses. He plundered her mouth, liking how hard he immediately got. She had him ready in a heartbeat, even if he wasn't planning on using that particular part of his body. No other woman turned him on this fast, for he'd never been as connected to anyone as he was to Scarlett.

The only reason he stopped kissing her was someone behind him honked, and he and Scarlett laughed as they drove away. She kept her hand on his leg the entire ride home. He drove into the garage, turned off the engine, hit the remote and leaned across the console for her again. He held her head tenderly between his hands as he kissed her mouth. He slid his hands into her hair and freed it from the pins. Her hair tumbled down around her shoulders, and he moved a strand or two away as he inserted a finger under the scoop of her dress and drew out her left breast. He shifted so he could bring his lips to the peak that waited so eagerly. He loved tasting her. She held his head close to her breast as he licked, swirled his tongue over the nub before returning to draw the nipple farther inside his mouth. He liked how sensitive she was.

He could feel her quiver. He used his free hand and bunched up the dress that didn't have far to go. Found the thin strip of fabric. Slid his finger along her wetness and made her head thrash. She swiveled, giving him even more access and he took that same finger and slid it inside. Then he brought his finger out before sending it back inside again. He repeated the motion until her legs shook and she came.

"I'm going to taste you," he told her as he lifted his head. He took his finger and put it in his mouth. "Delicious." He pulled her dress back down. "I'm going to lick you until you come in my mouth. Do you want that?"

Scarlett could only nod. Brad smiled. "Good. Tonight we're not stopping."

Her voice was deep and throaty. After what he'd just done, she wanted all of it. "No. No, we're not."

The light inside the garage flashed off, plunging them into darkness. "Shall we go inside?"

He came around to her side of the car. Lifted her into his arms. Carried her across the backyard and into the house.

She stood in the kitchen as he rearmed the alarm. Watched him shed his overcoat. The man was a siren in a suit. He held his arms out. "Come here."

"I want to seduce you," she told him, stepping forward.

"You already have. But I want to kiss you for a while." He brought his mouth to hers, making kissing an act all its own. His lips gently traced hers, as if memorizing every texture and nuance. His tongue slid inside to mate with hers, starting a dance that both knew where it would end.

The kiss was sweet yet sensual all at the same time.

"Do you know how beautiful you are?" he asked as he lowered his mouth to her collarbone. "I'm going to show you." He let her go and shed the suit jacket. Drew her back into his arms. "Now I can hold you closer. Kiss you better."

How was it possible that the next kiss topped the first? But it did, and as the passion grew between them, she needed to touch him. She'd wrapped her arm around him, and she moved her fingers to his tie. Tugged at the knot, pulled it loose and slid it from his neck.

Then she began undoing the buttons of his shirt, remained mesmerized as the white oxford broadcloth disappeared, revealing his undershirt. She slid it up and over, and it joined the dress shirt somewhere on the floor. "I peeked at the calendar," she admitted as her hands found bare skin. "You're much better in the flesh."

She ran her hands over his rock-hard abs. Traced the lines between the muscles. He gritted his teeth. Swore.

"So, tattoos?" she asked, moving around the back side of him.

"None," he admitted. "No identifying marks preferred in my SEAL work, and then once out, I never had the urge. I don't like needles."

"Ah, Mr. Big and Strong and Wonderful has a weakness."

"And I'm not afraid of admitting it," he replied. He sucked in his breath. Made it hiss out as she stood in front of him. She grabbed his belt loops and pulled him toward her. Took her hands and ran them down the front of his jeans. Cupped him. He grabbed her hands. Brought his mouth to hers.

"Love this dress, but it needs to go."

"It does." He leaned, and in a swift movement, he had her in his arms. He carried her up the back stairs as if she were light as a feather. Brought her into her bedroom and set her on her feet. Then he took her arms and lifted them above her head. He stripped the dress from her, then stopped and stared. She stood in her black stilettoes wearing only a lacy black bra and a tiny silk scrap of fabric.

"You are beautiful."

"You keep saying that."

"Only because it's true."

And as he kissed her again, Scarlett believed. She stood before him, no longer nervous or scared. She was a thousand and one nerve endings, all working together in harmony for one purpose—to be as close to him as possible. "Touch me," she demanded, emboldened by the desire pooling between her legs. He reached for her breasts, cupped underneath them and brought his mouth to the lace of her bra. He'd tasted her before, but now he took his time, lavishing attention on each peak until she strained against him. Her legs shook and her head fell back as her bra disappeared and his tongue found her unimpeded. She clung to his shoulders for support.

"I'll buy you new ones," he whispered, and he grabbed the thin fabric strap that sat on her right hip. It snapped as he tugged, and the thong joined the dress somewhere on the floor. A finger slipped lower and between her folds. Her body clenched around him. He slid his finger out, joined it with a second and slid both back in. She climaxed immediately and cried out. She'd wanted sparks and instead gotten fireworks, and they weren't even at the main event.

"Must taste you," he told her, dropping to his knees before her so he could put his mouth to her apex. He took a deep breath as if memorizing her scent. "So lovely." Then using his hands, he spread her legs and his tongue shot forth.

The moment he first slid his tongue across her wetness, Scarlett again had to hold on. She ran her fingers into his hair, clutched him to her as his tongue darted inside to drink. She wobbled on the stilettoes. "So beautiful," he repeated, kissing the inside of her thigh before going back. Another earth-shattering orgasm began to build as Brad's fingers spread her folds so his tongue could go deeper into the most intimate part of her. He suckled and she cried out. Tried to remain on two legs as her knees threatened to buckle. Fingers joined tongue as he feasted, and Scarlett, who'd desired for so long to do nothing but feel, let Brad's magic take her away. "Take it," he whispered. "Come. I'm going to make you come all night. Let go. Let go for me."

Never had such an intimate moment given her so much pleasure. Her having an orgasm was a destination in itself, not just some foreplay. The difference astounded her, and her legs shook and quaked as she came standing up, over the man whose mouth opened beneath her catching every drop. She held on for life as he refused to let her orgasm subside, his touch continuing to give her the longest orgasm ever. She felt engorged. Full. Satisfied. Pleasured completely. "So good," she told him, hearing the wonder and satisfaction in her voice.

And there would be more. They were only getting started. He leaned her back so her knees connected with the bed and she sat. Flopped back, spent. His hands slid down her legs and began to remove her shoes. Then he lay down next to her.

"I always want it to be good for you," he told her and she heard the conviction that told her she mattered to him, that those earlier words of love hadn't been a fluke.

"Went beyond good. That was incredible."

His finger slid around to the front and he caressed her nipple. "You have to tell me how you're doing. I don't want to make you sore."

"Don't you dare stop. In fact, you have too many clothes on."

"Tonight's not about me. Not until much later. If I don't keep my pants on, it'll be over way too fast."

She touched his chest. "Okay. Then I'm glad we have all night."

"I want to savor everything. It's been a while."

"For us both," Scarlett amended, gasping as his mouth found her nipple and her back arched to meet him. He kissed her, the sensation of mouth and skin highly erotic and charged. Yet, her subconscious could sense how cherished she was. His exploration was about her. He'd stop if she said the word. She could send him back to his apartment over the garage all hot and bothered and he'd go without protest. That fact allowed her to let go of any fear. She trusted him.

If Brad didn't realize how special he was, then the man was dense as fog. She put her free hand on the hand he used to caress her breast. Sighed as his tongue swirled around her, fulfilling her wish.

She had no idea how long he made love to her breasts. He pushed both together so he could take them at the same time. She cried out. The ache between her legs he'd satisfied earlier came back tenfold. Yet his mouth concentrated only on her breasts. Both hands and fingers. She reached to touch herself. Pulled back.

That caught his attention. He lifted, and her body ached for his touch. "Never hesitate to indulge yourself," he told her. "Do you know how sexy it is that you'll take your own pleasure?"

Her hand tentatively went back between her legs. He watched her do it. "Rub yourself."

She made a circle and he groaned. Looked at her with deep chocolate eyes. Her head dropped back. "Now, you do that and let me do this. I want you to come. You can't do this to yourself."

"No," she gasped as his mouth found her breasts again. "Oh shit!" She trembled violently as another extreme orgasm powered over her. Her breathing came hard and heavy and after she climaxed, she clutched the sheets with both hands. "Holy hell."

There was just enough light coming in around the curtains to put a faint glow in the room. She swore she could see him grinning from ear to ear. "That was incredible." He took one of her free hands and guided it to the bulge at the front of his pants. "Feel what you do to me."

"Oh." She rubbed her palm along the length of it. Oh boy. "You need to get naked," she told him. She found the fly and tugged.

His hand stilled hers. He seemed nervous, and the fact touched her deeply. "You sure?"

She tugged the second button. "Whatever you do . . . Don't. You. Dare. Stop."

Brad had gotten under her skin—okay, poor analogy considering the circumstances, but as he kissed her neck, she realized she wanted all this and more. They would deal with whatever the morning brought once the sun came up. For tonight, only the two of them—in this room—existed. No one else. No baggage. No memories. No comparisons.

Just the now.

She pushed him onto his back and freed the last button. Having already kicked off his socks and shoes, he lifted his hips as she stripped him of his jeans and boxers. She rose, went to the curtains and pulled them open another four inches. More streetlight slivered in through the narrow crack. He lay on the bed, watching her, his arms folded behind his head as she crossed the room, oddly not shy that she was completely exposed to him. "Condom is in my wallet," he told her.

"Won't need it. I never stopped taking the pill." She straddled his thighs. His hardened cock jumped. "Not unless you're diseased."

"Hell no. Took the tests and all. And two plus years," he reminded her.

"I know. I'm very impressed by that. It makes this all mine." Boldly she took his length in her hand. Closed and made a fist. Savored the pulse that throbbed in her palm. Heard his gasp as she stroked.

"Witch," he called to her.

"You ain't seen nothing yet," Scarlett teased. She moved her hand from base to tip, memorizing the feel of his soft, smooth skin. She took her thumb and ran it over the head, spreading the drop of pre-cum. She bent over and took the tip in her mouth. As she did she closed her eyes. Blotted out the past. After Todd had cheated, she'd refused. Simply couldn't go there. Do this. But this was Brad. An overpowering need to give him this gift overtook her and she swirled her mouth over him, savoring the musky flavor that was all his. Heat pooled. Oh, she'd missed this. Missed this connection. Was so glad she could share it with him.

He twitched in her mouth, and she smiled, heady with the pleasure only she could provide. She wanted him at the point of no return. She wanted to know—no, make that needed to know—that she could bring him to the edge and then take him further, as he had her, and that this was special. She lowered more, drawing him fully into her mouth. And loved it.

Loved him deeply and truly. The realization was

empowering. Freeing. Exciting.

He hit the edge. "Enough or I'll . . ." he said, grasping for her. "We should be together. I want us together."

She moved her mouth. Lifted herself forward and settled herself down. Sighed and shook as her body took him in. Adjusted to the sweet, blissful intrusion. He locked his gaze on hers and reached for her waist. Helped lift her up and down as she rode him. She leaned over his chest and his head came off the pillow so he could kiss her. She lost herself then to their connection, to their heat and friction. Passion carried her away—every pore alive. With every thrust, her awareness of what was coming heightened. Like the clicking of a roller coaster as it climbed, she could feel her orgasm building. Her hands clutched the sheets as every nerve ending began to sing in a rhythm as old as time. Then, as she reached the top, the orgasm began. She flew with it, up and over and up and over again until finally the thrill ride subsided and the ride ended. Still joined, she lay on his chest, breathing heavy. He stroked her back. Held her close. She'd never felt so secure. So safe. So unhurried. So loved.

His fingers traced circles on her skin. She didn't want to move, but finally, she slid off him and over to one side. His arm wrapped around her and she put her head on his chest, just below his shoulder. He drew the sheet around them. "Take a catnap," he told her. "You'll need your energy."

She was completely satiated. Spent. Yet his words had made her quiver, made her realize she could be ready to go again in a snap. "Can't wait for more."

He dropped a kiss on her forehead. "Don't worry. We're just getting started. That was only round one."

***

After five, or was it six, or maybe seven rounds, Scarlett woke. Sunlight flickered in around the curtains and through the gap she'd made. The beam hit her directly in the face, and as she shifted, she heard a muffled oomph. Worn out from a long night with little sleep, Scarlett found herself momentarily disoriented. She sat up. Grabbed the sheet to cover her nakedness. Turned to the man sleeping soundly next to her, his legs too long for the bed. Remembered that Colleen was at Jenni's and wouldn't come walking in the door.

She took a deep breath to calm her nerves. She didn't have regrets. Just no clue what to do from here. She glanced at the bedside clock. A little after nine. Now what? Did she get up and go about her day? Did she make him breakfast? She looked at him again. His brown eyes were open, staring up at her. "You look like you've seen a ghost. You okay?"

"No," she replied honestly.

He reached to stroke her cheek. "What's wrong?"

This was Brad. She had to be honest. "I have no idea what to do next."

He continued to trace the side of her face. "There's no wrong answer. I'll leave whenever you want me to."

"I don't necessarily want you to leave. But, I've never

been here before."

Brad had. Far too many times. Climb out of bed, get dressed, do a kiss on the cheek and find the door. That simple. His cheek itched and he scratched the stubble he'd need to shave. The amount of times they'd made love last night meant he knew she was sore. "How about we each get a shower and meet in the kitchen? I'll cook you breakfast."

Green eyes blinked relief. "Okay." Then she stared. "Do you mean shower together?"

He cupped her chin. Brought his lips to hers and gave her a kiss. "Not this time or I might take you against the wall. While I'd like that, you're sore."

"I am," she admitted.

"So I'll use the hall bath where all my stuff is. There's supposed to be more than enough hot water for each of us to take showers at the same time. If not, we'll find out and I'll add it to my fix-it list."

She nodded. "Okay. That sounds like a plan." She let the sheet slip as she rolled over.

He climbed out of bed, scooped up his clothes and strolled down the hall. About a half hour later he was clean, shaved and dressed. He headed back into the bedroom. Scarlett's bathroom door remained closed. She stepped out in nothing but a towel. "You're already dressed. I'm . . ."

He loved the way her face flamed to the color of her hair. Liked how the color spread down over her chest and to the tips of her breasts. Hell, he loved everything about her. "Guys move faster. I wanted to be here when you came out."

"Good, because every time we'd touched before you didn't come around for a few days. I'm not embarrassed by what we did. Just worried you might run out."

He walked around the edge of the bed and took her into his arms. "I won't do that again. Last night makes me want you more. Love you more. I meant what I said."

Her arms wrapped around him, stretching the long-sleeve T-shirt she'd put on. "This is still new to me, but I want this."

"I've liked you for over fifteen years. Since freshman year. I'm just as afraid as you are of what happens if it goes south."

She blinked rapid fire. "I guess I never looked at it that way."

"I know I've probably been a night and day asshole. Pulling you close and then afterward pushing you away. I was afraid. But I wouldn't have made love to you last night if my head weren't finally on straight. I want to have an us, but I'm as clueless as you are as to where we go next. I've never been in love, or if I have, it's not what I'm feeling for you. I'm hoping we take it one step at a time and it all works out."

"That's the only way I've known," Scarlett admitted.

"Then let me cook you breakfast," Brad offered.

"I'd like that. And you're okay with the package deal?"

Brad laughed and drew her into his arms. She felt so right there, like she'd been made to belong there. "I painted part of my house pink before you even arrived. Trust me, I love your daughter. You are a pair. Wouldn't have it any other way."

He led her down to the kitchen. He'd already cleaned up the articles of clothing he'd shed there last night. "What can I make you?"

"What can you cook?"

"I can make a mean omelet."

"Then show me."

Brad was still at her house hours later when Jenni brought Colleen home after lunch.

"Adam and the kids are in the car or I'd stay and catch up," Jenni said as Scarlett opened the front door. Jenni stepped into the foyer and passed over Colleen's princess suitcase. Brad came around the corner and reached for it. With his other hand, he boosted Colleen up onto his arm. "Brad!" Colleen said, giving him a kiss.

"Let's go get you unpacked," he said. "I'm sure Harry wants to play."

"Brenna has two cats," Colleen told him. "When can we get Harry a friend?"

"You'll have to ask your mom that question," Brad deflected, winking at Scarlett as he carried Colleen up the stairs.

"Great, another animal," Scarlett said.

"You knew it would only be a matter of time," Brad called back.

Jenni's chin tilted as she tracked them until they were out of sight. She gripped Scarlett's hands. "You did it."

"I'm very tired this morning," Scarlett confirmed.

Jenni's grin split wide. "About time. I can't wait to hear

all the juicy details." Adam honked the horn and Jenni rolled her eyes. "I'll text you later. Maybe we can have you all over for dinner next weekend or something. The guys can watch hockey on TV."

"What about hockey?" Brad asked as he came back downstairs. "She's unpacking and be prepared for the next kitten question. She's gearing up."

"Jenni invited us to her house next weekend for dinner and hockey. On TV."

"Sounds fun," Brad agreed.

The horn blared again. "That man is going to be the death of me," Jenni said with another eye roll. She gave Scarlett a hug. "Talk to you later."

Scarlett locked the door behind her. Turned around and arched an eyebrow. "You up for hockey and dinner?"

"Is that what couples do?"

She folded her arms. "Well, it's not bar hopping at our age. That requires a babysitter. I think the deal is we go hang out with other couples. With kids."

"Then I'm up for it." He reached forward and drew her to him. Pulled her arms apart and wrapped them around his waist. Leaned down and kissed her nose. "I want to be a couple with you."

"I want that too," Scarlett said, for she truly did. More than anything this felt right. "But we're going slow."

"Meaning?"

"I don't want to keep us a secret," she said, stepping out of his embrace so she could keep a clear head. "But I don't want to be in people's faces either. I want our relationship reveal to be gradual. Like they suddenly don't remember a day we weren't together. They'll realize it's been in front of them all along that we're together."

"What do we tell Colleen?"

"I'll figure it out," Scarlett said. "She loves you already. You're always here. Telling her we're dating won't mean anything to her. She's too young. So we'll cross that bridge when you move in."

He arched an eyebrow. "I'm moving in?"

Scarlett nodded. "Well, it is your house. Eventually I'd say that's going to be a logical step if things progress. And be prepared for when she tells my mom she's seen us kissing. That will be a moment too."

Brad drew back. "Okay. Are you trying to scare me like you tried before? I don't scare easily now. I'm tough. Faced down many a dangerous mission. How hard can this be?"

"How about when she decides you're her new daddy? Then you'll really be in the hot seat. Ready for that?"

Panic flickered across Brad's face. He masked it quickly. "Okay, maybe I'm a bit nervous. But it'll be okay. I agreed to that too when I signed on. And I'm in love with you. As long as you love me back, I'll be okay. I'm older. Wiser. I want to be with you," he emphasized with more conviction.

She could see how serious he was. "Good. Then we'll take this day by day."

"As long as we can take things night by night too." He wiggled his eyebrows Groucho Marx style to lighten the moment.

She laughed. "That will be a little bit trickier, but I'm sure we can figure that out too."

"Good, because last night was just a prequel."

"Really?"

"Mmm." He drew her to him and his lips nipped hers.

"Mommy," Colleen called.

She stepped out of his arms. "Duty calls. Be up in a minute, sweetheart."

Brad grabbed her hand and gave her one last tug. "I have some errands to run since I'm working tomorrow. How about dinner later? I'll bring carryout."

"Perfect," Scarlett said. "Can't wait."

She followed him to the back door. Gave him a lingering kiss and wished it could be longer. "I'll text you, so figure out what you'd like me to pick up," he said.

"Okay." She kissed him again and then he was through the door. A cold breeze filtered through. "Is it really going to snow again?"

"First of March and that's what they're saying," he said. "Hopefully this is the last cold snap. Keep warm and I'll see you later."

Later. Such a powerful word and one loaded with so much meaning.

With a smile, she went to see what Colleen needed.

Chapter Ten

Brad brought takeout from the King and I, one of the Thai places on South Grand. They ate their yellow chicken curry and vegetarian spring rolls at the center island. "Yummy," Colleen said. She rubbed her stomach. "My tummy is full."

"Good. Because you have a half hour to watch TV or read a book and then it's bath time," Scarlett said. "You also have to take care of Harry."

Colleen lifted her arms. "Brad, carry me upstairs."

"You can walk," Scarlett told her daughter. Colleen pouted and tromped up the stairs.

"She's going to be trouble with the boys when she gets older," Brad said. "That pout is killer."

"Which is why I want to thank you for not crossing me and for making her walk now."

"Not getting in the way of your parenting," Brad said, holding his hands up. "My mom didn't raise a fool."

"Nope and for that I'm grateful." Scarlett began to toss

the empty carryout containers. "This was a great idea. How much do I owe you?"

"Nothing."

"I do want to pull my own weight," Scarlett said. "I'm not a freeloader. There is some money coming in from the insurance annuity each month."

"Keep it. You can pay me back with kisses later."

"Hmm."

Brad recognized his mistake. "Yeah, that didn't come out right either. But I am going to kiss you later. Quite a few times actually."

"Next time I buy," Scarlett insisted.

"Fair enough." Brad sprayed the counter with disinfectant and began to wipe it down with a paper towel. "Hey, I found the perfect picture for the front hallway the other day. I picked it up when I was in between things today. I didn't have enough hands to carry it and the food. I'll go get it in a few minutes."

Colleen came back down the stairs. "Mommy, Harry pooped again."

"Yes, he has a way of doing that." Scarlett sighed and glanced at Brad. "He's a pooping machine."

"It's time she learned how to scoop," Brad told Scarlett. "How about I show her?"

"Okay. If you want, I can go to the studio and get the picture."

He paused with one foot on the stairs. "Sure. You can't miss it. The keys are in my coat pocket. Okay, Colleen. Let's go scoop poop. Time you did this yourself. Harry's not getting a friend until you are an expert at it."

Colleen giggled. "Okay."

Scarlett shook her head and laughed. Then she shrugged into her coat and retrieved his keys. While the snow was going to miss St. Louis and hit farther south, the temps had fallen into the teens. She crossed the backyard and climbed the stairs into Brad's tiny studio.

Situated under the roofline and with dormers, the ceiling sloped in places, making much of the space unusable. The result was a crammed room filled with a king-sized mattress and box spring, a small table, a dresser and the kitchenette unit. *No wonder he keeps all his stuff over at the house,* Scarlett thought.

She saw the picture leaning up against one of the table legs. Wrapped in brown paper and string, she wasn't sure what it was. As she picked it up, her gaze fell on the table and she paused. Under a magazine was some writing that looked a lot like—she moved the magazine—Todd's handwriting. The signature at the bottom confirmed it.

The letters were from Todd. Her fingers hovered. Twitched. Hesitated. Then she snatched the first one up. Read it from start to finish:

> *This is a heavy task to put on a bud, but we've been friends for too long to mince words. I've enclosed a letter for Scarlett. I need you to keep it until she's ready to see it. How will you know? When she finds someone and you think she's falling in love. I don't want her to be alone, but she's always so stubborn. She's too young for me to be the love of her*

entire life. That wouldn't be fair. As long as I have a piece of her heart, her love will be big enough for her to move on. Yeah, I've been gone too long, and probably haven't been there for her like I should. So she'll need someone to take care of her until she gets on her feet and I need you to do that for me. I know she'll be in good hands. Get her back to St. Louis where she belongs. You're there, you'll figure out how. Heck, maybe you'll be the one because I know you've always been sweet on her. I'd be okay with that, provided you treat her the way she deserves and not like all those other women who've flitted through your life. Who would have thought I'd be the married dude and you the playboy stud? Do me one favor, just make sure any man would be a great dad to my daughter. And don't let Colleen ever go a day without knowing how much I loved her. And stop blaming yourself. My decisions were always my own. Remember that. Todd.

Scarlett felt the tears begin to flow. Then she paused. Reread a sentence. What letter was for her? She reread the words, feeling more and more betrayed. There was a letter that Brad was supposed to give her. One he hadn't even told her about. One from Todd for her. She grabbed the next sheet of paper. Was this it?

Hey, only have a minute to scrawl something. Sending snail mail so I'm sure it gets there—don't trust those e-mail filters, you know? This next one looks dangerous. Got me thinking. Did I make the right choice? Maybe I should have bailed when you did. Okay, enough melancholy BS. I should start this over but no time. Don't worry. My head's in the game. I'll see you soon. But remember, if I don't, take care of Scarlett. Be there for her in the way I never was. Love her like I know only you can. Don't fail me, okay? Nah, you won't. You've always had my back. Todd.

There wasn't an envelope and the paper seemed to have been folded many times; it was wrinkled from being read over and over. She clutched the loose-leaf sheets in her hands. Automatically grabbed the paper-wrapped picture and carried everything out of the apartment.

Brad was waiting and he opened the back door. "Hey, I see you found it." He must have sensed something, for he immediately frowned. "What's wrong?" He took the picture from her fingers and as he did, the letters fell to the floor. He stepped back and set the picture on the island. "Oh."

"Oh." Scarlett made no move to pick them up. The worn white sheets lay like a defect marring the gray tile. "Were you ever going to tell me?"

"Tell you what?"

"That Todd gave you a letter for me. That he gave you those letters. Is that why you're doing all this for me? Because he asked you to?"

"No." But a hint of guilt had crept into his voice and she heard it. She frowned and grew angrier, zeroed in on what he'd said. "I wouldn't be in St. Louis if it weren't for you, for this house."

"I know."

He could see the betrayal on her face. Hated he'd put it there. "I care about you a great deal. I always have. I love you."

"Am I an obsession?"

"I've asked myself that many times. No, you aren't."

"What about our phone conversations? You played me and he'd asked you to do it."

"No."

"You made love to me," she accused.

"I made love to you because I love you. I wanted to tell you about the letters. I thought about breaking my promise. But I didn't. I promised him." Even to his own ears, the words sounded hollow. They were too little, too late.

"Then why keep these things from me? Why not tell me the truth? You haven't been honest with me from the start. I should have known there were letters. You should have told me."

"He told me one night in a bar he was sending me a letter for you. Just in case. Then I got that last note. They were his last wishes. I tried to follow them."

"So? When we became close, you should have told me. Where is my letter?" she demanded.

"In my locker at work. He asked me to give it to you when you're ready. When you were in love again. Don't you see the conflict I've been in? I've wanted you and he wanted me to take care of you."

"You took advantage of me."

"Maybe I did. I don't know." A hand raked through his hair, his agitation obvious. "I love you. Do you not understand my own guilt? I didn't have his back when he needed it most."

"You're making no sense."

Brad tried to make her see. "Because it's my fault he died."

"How can you say that? You weren't even there."

"If I'd reenlisted, I would have been there. I would have been on that mission. I could have had Todd's back. I could have saved him."

"You don't know that."

He raked a hand through his hair. "I don't know otherwise. Last night was a dream come true. You've always been the one for me. I knew it as far back as high school. I dated but only as a way to find someone, anyone, who could make me forget you. I never did. Then Todd died, and he wanted me to take care of you. Told me in as many words to love you like you deserved. I should have been there. I should have saved him. You deserve him, not me."

"You have to let the guilt go," Scarlett said, although in reality, she was reeling from all of the revelations. She'd spent one of the best nights of her life with Brad, making love and holding him in her arms, and he hadn't been fully open with her. Hadn't told her Todd had sent her a letter. Given her a message from the grave.

That felt like the worst betrayal. The question was if she could forgive him. If they could move past this. She slumped into one of the bar chairs. "You say you love me, but do you really love me because of who I am now or is your love just rooted in obsession, guilt and good sex?"

He appeared stricken.

"It doesn't matter," she told him briskly before he could speak. "I need time to think. And I want my letter. I don't care what Todd's directions say. I don't care what his final wishes were. I want it now."

He shook his head. "I'll bring it over Tuesday morning after my shift. It'll be the first thing I do. Unless you want to come by and get it?"

She didn't want to go to his work. See all his friends. She wouldn't put him through that awkwardness. "No. I need to think. Tuesday will be fine. We'll talk again then."

***

He was losing her. "Scarlett . . ." he began. He felt panic unlike any he'd ever experienced. His heart clenched and his breathing came out as a gasp. He'd lied when he said he was tough. Right now he wanted to cry like a baby; the thought of losing her scared him so.

Scarlett though was oddly calm. "Brad, I know you haven't been in a real relationship before, but when someone says she needs time, it means you give her that time. It doesn't mean we're over. It might, but it might not. I'm sorry, but you have to wait. I need to think things through. I want to take time to calm down and then I'm going to assess things. Then afterward, we'll talk. I promise you that we will talk. I live here and I'm not going anywhere. You won't come home and fine me gone. But for tonight, it's Colleen's bath time and I want you to go."

"Okay."

She nodded. "Thank you."

His heart broke. He wanted to reach for her, but knew that like when she'd given him time, he had to do the same. "Be sure to lock up and set the alarm."

"I will."

As Brad left, a blast of cold air swirled in, blowing the letters across the travertine tile floor. Behind him, she made no move to pick them up. The picture he'd bought for the front hallway remained unopened, like a bitter reminder that she'd never have found out about Todd's letters had she not gone to retrieve it. A chill stole over him and he sent up a silent prayer.

Brad carried the guilt of what had happened to work the next day. He could hardly concentrate. They were busy nonstop; the weather having coated the roads with a thin sheet of ice. By the time he'd worked his sixth car crash around the end of the evening rush hour, Brad wished people would have just stayed home. Either that or slow down. Like, way, way down.

He sat behind the wheel, grateful the interior of the fire truck was still warm for the drive back to the house. "Thought the temps would be in the twenties today. What's this single-digit crap?" Chris complained from the front passenger seat. "Road crews missed the boat on this one. At least we're done."

"I want to be a meteorologist. They screwed up too. Heck, you get paid six figures to stand on TV and be wrong. I want that job," Lewis added from the back.

The radio came to life and each man tensed as the dispatcher relayed their new assignment—a water rescue. Brad turned the siren back on and drove the fire truck to the dock. "Son of a bitch," Lewis cursed as they headed to the boat. "You shitting me? Didn't want to go in the Miss today. That water's going to be brutal. They need to start salting the tops of those barges. Why don't they salt the barges?"

"The river is still a damn ice field. They shouldn't have been moving. They should have tied up." Roger said as they suited up into the protective gear. He'd navigate the boat to the location where the man had gone overboard. They launched, and the windchill slapped all of their faces as they cut across the water at as high of a speed as possible. Brad shivered. Despite the heavy wetsuit, the wind was freezing.

They pulled up alongside the barge, both boats bobbing in the fast current. Brad gave a curse as chunks of river ice floated by, dangerous white islands illuminated by all the floodlights. He tethered himself and got ready to go in. He had a job to do and despite his tiredness, he wouldn't fail. A man's life depended on it.

Lewis would head into the water first and lead the way to where they thought the man was located. Given the water temperatures, they had only a short time to find him before hypothermia set in. "You got my back?" Lewis asked.

"Always," Brad said. It'd be the last thing he'd say that night.

***

Scarlett had no inkling anything was wrong. She only knew that by ten a.m. Tuesday morning, Brad hadn't shown up and brought her the letter. She fumed, but refused to look needy. Instead she took Colleen to the YMCA pool for her swimming lessons. Took her out to lunch as well, going back to Steve's Hot Dogs. Being stressed, Scarlett opted for one of their more adventurous choices of a chili cheese dog and finished the entire thing.

By three p.m., she was ready to blow a gasket and wanted to call Brad and find out why he was playing games with her. She checked her phone for the hundredth time. Nothing. He hadn't even had the courtesy to call or text. "I'm going to check on Brad," she told Colleen. "I'll be right back."

She walked out to the garage, opened the side door and found his SUV gone. She frowned and an uneasy feeling overtook her. "This makes no sense. He should be home. And he wouldn't ignore me."

She went back into her house, broke down and sent him a text message: *This is getting ridiculous. I thought we were going to talk,* she typed. *Where are you?*

Fifteen minutes later there was still no answer. But then her phone rang. She didn't recognize the number.

"Hello?"

"Is this Scarlett?" a woman's voice she didn't recognize asked.

She clutched the phone. Like when the men had come, she now realized something was terribly wrong. "Yes. This is she speaking."

"Hi Scarlett. I'm Ellen Silverman."

"Brad's mom." Scarlett gripped her cell phone tightly.

"Yes. There's been an incident. I would have called you earlier, but Brad's phone is locked. Your number just came up on the screen and I saw it and dialed."

Scarlett froze. She opened her mouth but no words came. Fear overtook her and rendered her mute.

"Brad's going to be fine," Ellen quickly went on, "so don't worry. He's at the hospital for observation. I'm here with him. I hope you don't mind that I took the liberty of calling and telling you."

"No, no. I'm glad you called." Scarlett tried to breathe. Her chest heaved. Panic clutched her. "Can you tell me what happened?"

"He was out on the river doing a rescue. Took close to four hours. They're treating him for hypothermia and frostbite. His dad and I are here with him."

Scarlett's phone began to beep. Her mother. She ignored the call. "Where is he?"

"Barnes. But he's sleeping right now. Has been for a long time. The doctors say he'll be released soon and this is just standard procedure. I'll call you again. The nurse is here and I have to go."

Scarlett's phone began to vibrate again as her mother tried again. She answered. "What?"

"I just got one of those news alerts on my phone. They reported two firefighters were hurt during a water rescue late last night. They didn't give names or details, just that they'd been taken to the hospital. Said they were with the marine unit. Is it Brad? Was he working?"

"Did they say what injuries?" Scarlett wanted to know if there was more Ellen hadn't told her.

"The news didn't say. It actually gave very little information. Rather shoddy reporting if you ask me. Is Brad okay?"

"Mom, can you come get Colleen? I need to get to Barnes."

"It's Brad?" Her mom's voice inched upward. "Oh, honey. Is he alright?"

"Mom." Scarlett couldn't believe how calm her voice was. Inside she was a quivering batch of nerves. "Mom, his mother called. Said he's okay. But I'm going. How about I bring Colleen to your house? We can be there in about fifteen minutes."

"Oh, honey. Don't disturb her. I'll have your father drive. He's good in a crisis. We're on our way."

"Okay," Scarlett said. She went upstairs and found Colleen brushing Winnie's hair. Harry was batting a toy mouse around the room. "Colleen, I have to go out for a little bit. Granny and Grandpa are coming to play with you."

"Okay," Colleen said.

Scarlett went into her bedroom and changed out of her sweats. She put on a sweater and jeans. Tamed her hair into a tight knot.

Thirty minutes later, Scarlett hurried up to the information desk at Barnes-Jewish Hospital. "Brad Silverman's room," she said.

The woman looked it up and directed her to the correct elevator. Scarlett reached the floor and found the nurses' station. "I'm here for Brad Silverman," she told them.

Two men sitting in a waiting area stood. "Scarlett?" one of them asked. "I'm Lieutenant Chris Ames. This is Roger Pyle. Remember, from the cookies?"

"Is Brad okay?" She wrapped her arms around her waist.

"Yeah, but I'll be busting their chops. He and Lewis needed to come out of the water, but they refused because they were so close to rescuing the victim. Stubborn ass . . . Sorry." He appeared mortified at his outburst. "My apologies. My guys mean a lot to me."

"Understood. I was married to a military man. No offense taken. So," she prompted.

"They got him, but we had to send in another set of guys to pull all of them out. Then there's the journey back. Anyway, they were treated for frostbite and hypothermia and held for observation. We're not letting them out of here until they're one hundred percent. Doctor says that's soon, so we came back up to wait. Doc also said that they were very lucky. No permanent damage."

"The guy they rescued is also going to make it," Roger added.

Relief filled Scarlett. "Can I see him?"

"Yeah. It's that room over there." The lieutenant pointed her in the right direction.

"Thanks."

The door was cracked, and she pushed it open. After passing the bathroom and the closets, she stepped into a double room. Both beds were occupied. An older woman held the hand of the man in the first bed. She glanced up as Scarlett went by. Scarlett stepped to the edge of the curtain and looked around. Hospital beds had a way of making anyone look small, and the larger-than-life Brad Silverman was no exception. Upright slightly, she could see how pale his face was. He was hooked up to monitors and an IV drip. He was covered with warm blankets that came up to his chin, both arms underneath and to his sides. Nothing but his face was visible.

"Scarlett?" Ellen glanced up from her vigil. "You're here."

The woman by the next bed rose. "Scarlett?" She came around the corner and drew Scarlett in for a big hug. "It's going to be okay. I'm Peggy, the cat lady. That fool over there is my Lewis. We've been married a long time or I'd kill him for this. They're going to be fine. Lewis might lose the tips of his fingers, but that's all. He took the worst of it. Told me Brad had his back, which is why he's even alive. Could have been so different. Brad saved him. Held him tight while the other guys pulled him out."

Scarlett had thought she could handle this. She began to shake. Tears began to stream down her face. "I . . . I . . ."

Peggy patted her on the back. "I know. It's going to be fine. He's going to be fine. How's that kitten?"

"Fine," Scarlett said, but Peggy's diversion failed. "What was he thinking?"

"They're rescuers. It's what they do. They saved the man's life and Brad refused to leave Lewis. My husband took on too much. Thinks he's Superman but he's not. Luckily Brad was there."

Scarlett trembled. "I thought I could do this."

She had. Todd had been overseas. Out of sight was pretty much out of mind. That fact had made all his missions bearable. After that first year of marriage, she'd learned to stop worrying if his calls or Skype sessions came long after he'd promised. Something always came up. He'd always had an excuse and laughed away her fears.

"Come with me," Peggy soothed, and she guided Scarlett out into the hall. She gave her another hug and when they drew apart, she leaned in close to Scarlett. "Do you love that man in there?"

"My husband was military. He died in action. I was so angry with Brad the other day for something he did. Now it seems so stupid. So petty. I'm a horrible person. I cussed him when he didn't come this morning like he promised."

"Next time, you'll be his emergency contact. I'll tell Chris to make sure Brad gets it done."

"No, his mother . . ."

"Is a lovely woman, but Brad loves you. I've heard all

about you from Lewis. He says Brad talks about you all the time. Heck, he adopted a cat because of you and your daughter. Lewis said they really didn't have to twist his arm much." Peggy didn't let go of the vise grips she had on Scarlett's arms. "Do you love him?"

"Yes." The word ripped from deep within. When faced with the fact she could have lost Brad forever, Scarlett realized the truth she'd been afraid to acknowledge. "But, I'm scared. How do I go through this again?"

"You just do if you love him. You could walk out of here and be in a car accident. The news is filled with stories of bad things that shouldn't happen, but they do and they are simply senseless. We can live in fear, or we can live each moment we have to the fullest. If you do that, you'll always have enough days. You'll never feel you ran out of time."

"Scarlett?" Ellen stood in the doorway. "He's awake and he's asked for you. Why don't you go in? I'm going to get some coffee. Find my husband. He hates these places."

Peggy gave Scarlett one last smile and loosened her grip on Scarlett's arms. "Remember what's really important."

She didn't need to say the word for Scarlett to know it was love.

Scarlett followed Peggy back into the room and walked into the back section of the room. Brad's eyes were open. "Hey."

"Hi," she said. She went over to him and dropped a kiss on his forehead.

"I'm sorry I didn't get home."

"That doesn't matter right now. I'm just glad you're okay."

"I must look like a mess." He attempted a laugh. It came out as a cough.

"It's like they put you in a papoose," Scarlett said, describing the way his covers were tucked all around him.

"I'll get you your letter once I get out of here."

She shook her head. "It can wait."

"I promised I would. I keep my promises."

That's how much he loved her, Scarlett realized. Even now he put her first. "Your health is more important than a letter. You are more important," she repeated to drive the point home. "There are things we need to talk about, but not here. Not now." Her eyes welled up with fresh tears.

"Don't cry," he told her. "Please don't be sad."

"Don't scare me again," she told him, wiping the tears away.

"Tell that to my doctor. He's been overdramatic. I'm fine."

"Hardly," Scarlett scoffed. "And you say I'm stubborn. Pot calling the kettle black."

"Touché," Brad said. He smiled wanly. "I'm not going anywhere. I promised Todd I'd take care of you."

She wiped the last tears away. "How about you promise me that you'll take care of me? Don't promise Todd. Promise me. And then I'll promise to do the same for you."

He closed his eyes, still clearly exhausted. Took a breath. Opened them again. "I can do that. I'd like to do that."

"The next time we talk, you're going to do just that. Understand?" Urgency filled her until he nodded. "Good. Until then, you get better."

"Yes, ma'am," Brad whispered. "Now go home."

"I'll stay as long as I want," Scarlett argued. "I love you and you're not getting rid of me that easily."

Brad tried to smile. "Always so stubborn. Then stay. But I'd rather you be with Colleen. And the faster you go, the faster I can get out of this place, because I want to be with you, and you won't be here."

"Such faulty logic. But I'll concede. This time. Only because I love you."

"My one win."

"Yep. Don't get used to it." She leaned over and kissed his lips, the kiss light and tender and full of love. "You'll stay in the house when you come home. Don't even think of going upstairs to your apartment."

He closed his eyes. "Yes, ma'am. See you soon."

"Yes, you will, my love."

As Scarlett strode from the room, Peggy gave her a thumbs-up. Scarlett ran into Ellen and Aaron on the way back toward the elevator. Ellen shifted a coffee cup and held out her hand. Scarlett took it and she squeezed it.

"Sorry to scare you earlier," Ellen said. "You didn't have to come all the way down here, but I'm glad you did. Kids. You know what they say. You never have an uneventful day ever again once you have them."

"True," Scarlett agreed. She could tell she and Ellen

were going to be good friends.

"We'll get to know each other better under better circumstances," Ellen said. She squeezed Scarlett's hand again. "I can tell you're not going anywhere."

Scarlett smiled and shook her head. "No, I'm not."

Ellen nodded. "Good. He's liked you for a long time. You make him happy."

"He makes me happy too. I'd stay, but he's being too macho for his own good."

Ellen sighed. "My son the hero. Always saving people."

Scarlett reached her hand out and placed it on Ellen's arm. Her next words came from her heart and were the absolute truth. "Well, don't worry. I'm here now and I'm going to save him right back."

***

Brad's parents brought him home about two hours later. His dad had retrieved Brad's SUV from the fire station, and his mom had followed in hers. Once they had Brad inside, his parents didn't stay. They were in and out in less than five minutes. "We'll keep his siblings away," Ellen told Scarlett before she left. "I can buy you at least a day before they descend to check on him themselves."

"You'll get to meet everyone," Brad grumbled. "Pain in the butt, all of them."

"Someone's crabby," Scarlett said good naturedly. "Let's get you back to bed."

He frowned. "I'm fine. I hate lying around. I'm not an invalid. I should have been treated and released."

"Better safe than sorry," Scarlett reinforced. "Upstairs with you and I'll bring you some hot cocoa. I'll even let you stay up and watch *Frozen* with Colleen. How can you resist that since you literally were frozen?"

Beaten, Brad sighed and shrugged out of his winter coat. A folded manila envelope fell onto the gray tile. His body was stiff, so she retrieved it. "What's this?"

"Your letter is inside."

The envelope was addressed to Brad at his parents' Flora address. "I thought it was in your locker?"

"I moved it to my car at the start of my shift. Didn't want to forget it. Luckily I did, given what happened." He was still worse for wear—exhaustion etched into the new lines covering his face. He needed rest.

Her fingers held the thin envelope, assessing its heavy coarse texture. Then she tossed it unopened onto the center island. "The letter isn't what's important now. You are. Let's go. Get upstairs."

Proving how worn down the ordeal had made him, Brad went up the stairs without further argument. When she brought up the hot chocolate, complete with whipped cream, she found him cuddled together with Colleen under her favorite fuzzy throw blanket. On the screen, the character Elsa was singing "Let it Go." Scarlett passed over the mugs. Knowing Colleen would immediately take a drink, Scarlett had added an ice cube to hers. "Yours is hot," she told Brad. "Be careful."

He nodded, and the group fell into an easy silence, disturbed only by Colleen's occasional chatter as she pointed out something in the movie. After the movie ended, Scarlett put Colleen to bed. "Brad's going to stay here," she told her daughter. "He's going to move into the house. Is that okay?"

"Yes," Colleen enthused. "I love Brad."

"I know you do." Scarlett kissed her daughter on the forehead. Harry had curled up next to her and was already asleep. "Brad loves you too."

"So will we be a family?" Colleen asked.

Scarlett turned off the light and the night light came on. "Yes, we will."

"Good," Colleen said, snuggling under the covers. "I like that idea."

Scarlett returned to the living room, where Brad had spread out on the couch. He was fast asleep. She sighed. She'd meant for him to sleep in the bed with her. He wasn't going to be comfortable if he stayed here. She shook his shoulder. "Brad."

"Huh?" he asked.

"You're not sleeping here on the couch."

"No?" he grumbled, barely awake.

"No," she repeated.

She helped him to his feet and led him into her bedroom. Their bedroom, she corrected. She wasn't planning on letting him go ever again. Brad stripped down to his boxers and climbed into the queen-sized bed. They'd need to move his mattress and box spring in, Scarlett noted, so he fit better. "Do I need to get you up for work?"

"No," he mumbled. "Don't work until at least Friday. Have to get cleared by workman's comp doc first before I can report. Appointment's written on my dismissal paper."

"Then get some rest," she told him. "I'll be back in a little bit after I clean up the hot cocoa cups."

She leaned over him and watched as he closed his eyes. She turned off the bedside lamp, bathing the room in darkness. She stood still, waiting until she heard the regular breathing that indicated he was asleep. Then she went back out to the living room and carried the dirty hot chocolate mugs to the kitchen. She put them in the dishwasher, along with the dinner dishes. The elephant in the room sat on the island, and she reached for the manila envelope. Her fingers fumbled with the metal clasp and she broke one of the metal prongs as she opened the flap.

Inside was a plain white number ten envelope. Todd had scrawled her name across the front. The envelope was the old kind—meaning Todd had had to lick the glue strip in order to seal it. She could tell no one had ever opened it.

She started to slide a shaking forefinger under the edge and then changed her mind and used a steak knife. Like the previous letters to Brad, Todd had written hers on lined loose-leaf paper. Unlike Brad's, hers was still crisp and clean from only having been folded once.

She unfolded the trifold missive, took a deep breath, and sat on one of the counter stools. She could do this. She could read Todd's final words to her.

My beloved Scarlett, he began. She closed her eyes and

set the paper down. Then she tilted her face heavenward so she could stare at the high white ceiling. She took a few deep breaths before lifting the paper again. There was nothing to be afraid of but fear itself, right?

My beloved Scarlett. If you're reading this, first, it means that I'm no longer here. I'm sorry for putting you through that. No one plans to die, and no one plans to hurt anyone, especially the ones they love. I'm sorry for the pain and loss. I never meant to ever hurt you, ever. But if you are holding this, then it means Brad's determined you've fallen in love again. Perhaps it's selfish of me, especially because I probably haven't been the best husband, more like an ass, really, but I wanted you to know that my final wish is that you are happy. That's all I ever wanted for you. Maybe we were too young and too naïve to know any better, but that's what made our love exciting, you know? I did love you very much. Do love you. You were my rock and I know I took you for granted. I hope whoever he is that he knows to never do that. You shouldn't take one minute for granted. Not one. I made that mistake and I don't want you to do the same. So don't mourn for me but grasp—what is it, that gold ring? Hell, it doesn't matter. Grab whatever it is, whoever it is, grab him with both hands and don't let go.

Scarlett set the letter down, went to the roll of paper towels, grabbed one and blew her nose. She used another to wipe her tears. Oh, Todd. There was more, but Scarlett couldn't read through the waterworks falling from her eyes. Tears dripped onto the white paper, but the aged ink long dried didn't smear. She wiped her eyes again and continued.

> *I hope he's a good husband to you. I've asked Brad to look out for you, so if he's giving you this then he's convinced that whoever you've chosen is the right person. He's always cared for you, so I know I can trust him in this. He's called me out every time I was a shit. I can trust him to be your champion and screen whoever comes around. Brad's always had my back, and he won't let anyone come around who's not worthy. Call it my last act from the grave, but you and Colleen are too important to leave this thing fully to fate. I hope you'll forgive me for meddling but understand why I had to do that. Last, I need you to do something for me. Brad didn't reenlist. If I'm gone, he's going to think it's his fault. That's just his way. He'll blame himself. He'll think he could have done something. Made it different. After my first tour, remember how we set up our estate? Seemed so premature and oh how we fought. But the fact is, like I told you, when your number's up, it's up. And if you're holding this, then my ticket got punched and nothing could have stopped that bitch fate from claiming her prize. So make sure you forgive him, and maybe that will help him forgive himself. I've told him, but he's not going to believe me.*

At this point, Scarlett noticed there were a few watermarks on the paper not caused by her own tears. Todd had been crying himself as he wrote it. Her super tough Navy SEAL had shed tears.

> *I'm sure by now I'm rambling as I write this, but I'm sitting here contemplating that I'm dead, which is something none of us want to ever do, and trying to think of everything I want to say to you that I haven't said over the years. How sorry I am when I hurt you. How you made me the happiest man in the world when you married me and how I could see heaven when you placed Colleen in my arms for the first time. I think I'll miss her growing up the most, for every time I come home she's changed. There's nothing like being Daddy, you know? I owe that to you. You're a fabulous mother. I know she's in good hands. And you, my love, I'll miss sitting on the beach with you and watching the sunset. That moment of orange and reds where the earth seems for a moment like it's on fire. There's nothing like California. Thank you for leaving me there but know that I am always with you in spirit. I have your back.*

A few more water droplets marred the ink, made the paper ripple. Scarlett needed another paper towel and pulled four large sheets off the roll. Might as well. She figured she'd use them.

> *I only have a few more minutes and I've got to get myself together. The guys don't need to see me like*

this. Just know I love you and I want you happy. Please go on with your life. Live. Laugh. Love. Like that sign in our house says. Take that to heart. You're not the type to forget, and I know you never will, but you are the type to hold on. You deserve to be happy, so let me go and move on. Let yourself love again and be happy. It's my final wish for you. Love you forever, Todd.

Scarlett set the letter down and let the tears flow. She cried for the loss. She cried for being able to finally let go. She sobbed for what should have been and for the foresight Todd had in making sure she knew she could have a future free from guilt. She lifted the letter and kissed the sheets of paper. Carried them into the living room where the flag sat like a beacon, the lone decoration in the darkened room highlighted by the glow of the streetlights. "I will always love you," she whispered, touching the glass. "Thank you. Thank you."

She heard the footsteps and the lights in the hallway flickered on. "Scarlett? Are you okay? Why do I have this feeling things aren't okay?" Brad hit the switch and the floor lamp flooded the room with light. He saw her tears immediately and crossed to her side. "Hey. What's wrong?"

"Why are you out of bed?" she asked, trying to hide her tears.

"I'm a former SEAL. I'm fine. You're not. Tell me."

She sniffled and extended the letter. "Here."

He didn't reach for it. "This is yours."

She waved it and the papers rustled. "It's okay. Please.

You need to read it."

Brad took it and she turned back to face the flag. She could see him reflected in the glass. When he finished reading, he looked at her. She simply nodded and burst into fresh tears. He gathered her into his arms, the letter in one hand. Then he reached behind him and set it on the mantel, freeing his hand. She pressed her face to his bare chest, inhaling. "Please forgive me," she begged.

"You have nothing to be sorry for," Brad told her. "I'm the fool. But I'm here and I'm not going anywhere."

"You scared me today. I was so angry. So afraid."

"I'm sorry. But I promise to be home after every shift. I'm going to sit on that porch with you when we are old and gray. I promise."

"I'm going to hold you to that. As well as a promise for no more guilt. No more running away. It wasn't your fault Todd died. I forgive you. He forgives you. You have to forgive yourself or we can't go forward. I want a future with you. Todd wants me happy, and you make me happy."

A lone tear slid down Brad's cheek. "Okay. I'll try. I've never done this before. It's all new."

She used two fingers to wipe away the tear. "I'll show you the way. I'll have your back the entire time. That's my promise." She put it in terms he'd understand. "My forever mission."

He lowered his lips to her and kissed her lightly. "It feels so wrong to be happy when he's not here."

"But he is. He's here." Scarlett put Brad's hand on his heart. Then she moved it to hers. "He's also here. And this is what he would have wanted," Scarlett soothed. "His last act of unselfishness was to bring us together, almost as if he knew it was the right thing to do. He loved us that much, and if we don't respect his gift by loving each other to the best of our abilities, for the rest of our lives, then we will have failed him."

"Let's not do that. I love you. I want us to be happy."

"We will because I love you too."

He kissed her again tenderly, and she took his hand and led him from the living room. As they went upstairs, they flipped the switches, sending the house into darkness. "Back to bed," Scarlett said, and Brad climbed onto the queen-sized mattress.

"I want a whole new set of furniture in here, so we'll need to buy a new bed," he told her as she returned from the bathroom. "Okay with that?"

"As long as I can find you in it," Scarlett said as she slid under the covers. He kissed her tenderly and then spooned himself around her, drawing her close so he could hold her tight. At that moment, the cuddling gesture was more intimate and full of promise than any sexual act could have been. "But what will I do when you sleep at the firehouse?"

"You can fill the bed with cats," Brad told her. "Or kids."

"Be careful what you're offering. I could take you up on both," Scarlett said with a joyous little laugh. He made her so happy. "If you don't watch out, you might get much more than you bargained for."

"I already have," Brad whispered against her neck as they drifted off into sleep. "I already have."

Epilogue

Eighteen months later

"Who gets married in their home?" Bernadette said, fussing with the white rose bouquet. She shooed Harry from the bed. Now fully grown, he strode out, tail high, followed by their newest cat, Cleo. "What was wrong with a church wedding? Or a reception somewhere nice rather than a barbeque in the backyard?"

"Mom," Scarlett chided gently. "This is what I wanted."

Scarlett gave herself one last glance in the floor-length mirror. The off-white dress was a simple, A-line silk sheath that fell to her knees. Her hair had been pinned up and had pearls woven through, and wispy tendrils of gold dropped onto her cheeks. "It's perfect and we wanted to show the place off. We've spent the last two years perfecting it and it's what brought us together in the first place. Besides, we wanted something simple. Just family and close friends."

"You're pretty, Mommy," Colleen said. She would act as the maid of honor.

"Let me fix your gloss," Scarlett said. She opened the tube and swiped Colleen's lips with another light pink layer. "Perfect."

Jenni came into the bedroom and gave Scarlett a thumbs-up. "We're ready."

Scarlett's mom gave her a big hug. Tears glistened in her eyes. "I'm so happy for you," she told her.

"Mom, you'll make me cry and ruin my makeup. Out." Scarlett gave her mom a kiss and wiped her eyes. "Go take your seat."

"We good to go?" Jenni asked. Scarlett nodded. "Then I'll go tell them."

The ceremony was in the first-floor living room, and as violin music began floating up the stairs, Scarlett took her daughter's hand. "You ready for this?"

"For you and Dad to be married? Yes." Colleen had started calling Brad *Dad* over a year ago. She paused. "Do you think Daddy in heaven is watching?"

Scarlett nodded. Touched the diamond earrings she wore in Todd's honor. "I do. And I think he's very happy for us."

"Me too."

So holding hands, she and her daughter began their descent down the staircase. When they made the turn at the landing, they could see into the living room and the guests assembled there. Brad's coworkers. Jenni, Adam and their kids. All of her and Brad's extended families on both sides. The only ones missing were Todd's parents, but Scarlett understood their decision not to postpone their trip to Argentina. They'd accepted the situation and wished her and Brad well, but today would have been hard for them.

Brad waited by the front windows—the guests were seated back through the living room and into the dining room where all had a great view. Brad wore his blue suit instead of the tuxedo. She'd wanted an informal ceremony, a complete contrast to the Vegas wedding she'd had after high school in which they'd all rented formal wear, including the gaudy, poufy white dress she'd worn.

She and Colleen approached, and at that moment, Brad looked up and smiled at her. She knew she'd never forget the love she saw in his eyes or the expression of undeniable joy on his face. Her entire heart warmed and filled with love. This was the official start of their future, as was the baby she was carrying that so far only Brad knew about. They'd tell everyone else later, over the wedding cupcakes, when they all realized she couldn't sip the celebratory champagne. She released Colleen's hand and gave her the bouquet to hold. Took Brad's hands in hers. "You ready for this commitment?" she teased.

He tightened his grip. Those brown eyes never wavered. "I've been waiting for this day my whole life."

She turned to the minister. "We're ready."

"Dearly beloved, we are gathered here today to join . . ." the minister intoned, beginning the ceremony.

And as Scarlett said her vows, sealing herself to the man she loved, the man who'd given her a second chance at happiness, the man she'd saved from himself in the process, the century-old house seemed to sigh—its future as a home for a loving, growing family forever secure.

Sneak Peek

One Suite Deal

Chapter One

It is a truth universally acknowledged, that a single woman in possession of a good job and who has her own money, must still be in want of a husband.

No offense to paraphrasing Jane Austen, but what Lana Winchester really wanted was to make it to her next plane, which was why she was running on two-inch heels through PDX.

She cursed the fact she hadn't changed into her favorite flats. After traveling for work the last two years, she considered herself an expert traveler who definitely knew better than to wear heels. But she'd wanted to look good for her last meeting, which had run over. She'd made it to the Eugene airport with razor-thin minutes to spare. Once aboard, her plane had sat on the tarmac.

And sat and sat while passengers with connecting flights, like Lana, kept glancing at their watches and wondering exactly when the plane would leave the gate and taxi toward the runway.

What was that about best laid plans? The first leg flight from Eugene had arrived late, putting her even more behind. Double curses to the airline app that told her she must check in with the gate agent in order to change her second flight. What good was technology if it didn't allow her to do things?

She had to get on this specific flight from Portland— Oregon, not Maine—so she could make it home to Beaumont before the big snow storm hit St. Louis and the entire Midwest. If not, she might not make it at all.

Everything had conspired against her today, including Mother Nature. If it hadn't been for a text from her mother telling her that the storm was moving in early, Lana would have been stuck in Oregon. If she didn't get on this exact plane, every later flight to St. Louis would be cancelled. The odds stood at one hundred percent.

One bright side? She had one of those tickets that allowed for no cost, same-day changes as long as seats were available. According to the app, there were two left.

While she liked her time working in Oregon, she had to get home. Normally she might not mind being stuck in such a pretty location, but her younger brother Ryan's eighteenth birthday was tomorrow. She had to be there.

With eight years between her and her sibling, she'd been in college before he'd even reached middle school. Engaged and disengaged before Ryan had started his freshman year. Now he was three months from graduating high school, and she refused to miss his birthday, especially as she'd already missed so many.

Even though they talked, with her constant travel, her brother was more a stranger than friend. She'd never seen him play high school basketball. He was a shooting guard on varsity, whatever that meant. In a recent video chat, her mom had told her he'd received calls from coaches as far away as Gonzaga in Washington State, Duke in North Carolina, and the University of Connecticut. Even the non-sports-watching Lana knew that meant her brother was good. He hadn't yet committed, preferring to wait until the end of the season and hopefully a state championship. His one birthday wish? That she attended at least one of his games. She had determined that she would be there, Mother Nature be damned.

Refusing to disappoint her brother or her family again, Lana double-timed it through the thick crowd and tried not to crash into any of her fellow travelers. Today was the first Saturday in March, so too early for the spring break travel crazy, but not too early for those who didn't understand airport etiquette meant they were supposed to stand to the right and walk on the left. She bypassed people on the speed walk, yelling "Excuse me" and ignoring their surprised or miffed glances.

Pushing through with the fastest power walk she could manage without triggering an asthma attack, she felt her quilted, waterproof tote bag slip from her shoulder, the computer inside clipping the arm of someone who didn't move out of the way soon enough. Without even looking back, she called "Sorry" and kept going.

Seriously, she could always tell the casual tourists who gave themselves hours to make their flight from the business travelers who knew how to get where they were going with better efficiency and far less luggage. Lana was in the latter group.

Once she'd taken the quality control job with Cederberg Interiors, she'd quickly learned how to ensure she fit two-weeks' worth of clothes in a hard-sided carryon. Her iPad and her laptop were in the tote on her shoulder, along with king size bag of peanut M&M's candy and a tall, thin bottle of Smart Water she hadn't opened on the previous leg.

While many might not find her job as an installation supervisor interesting, Lana loved the challenge. As someone who lived inside hundreds of hotel rooms a year and oversaw the renovations of the rest as her daily job, the work she did mattered. She was the final signoff after hotels upgraded their rooms and communal spaces. She ensured the decorative and installation work Cederberg Interiors performed exceeded expectations. In the case of Clayton Holdings, one of Cederberg's longest clients, the standards were exceptionally high. Clayton Hotels made luxury and service synonymous, indicative by their discerning clients and high number of repeat bookings.

Her next assignment was the first time her work would bring her home for an extended period. She'd be in Beaumont for at least a week, staying onsite at the

Beaumont Grand, the top-tier golf course resort hotel Clayton had opened last year as part of its master plan to revitalize the entire county. She'd be close to her family as she quality controlled the final finishing work on the Grand's neighbor—the smaller, pricier, and far more exclusive Chateau. The luxurious boutique hotel opened in April. Lana would double check the installations of the fixtures, the furniture—pretty much everything from floor to ceiling—before signing off on that Cederberg's part in the project was complete. She'd get to spend some quality time with her family. Even if she wasn't staying with them, she'd be in the same town and spend her nights visiting. Catch a game as Ryan wanted.

That was if she could get a seat on this plane.

The gate was just ahead, on the left, and Lana saw two attendants behind the counter. One agent appeared to be talking to a tall man who had his back to her. Unlike him, Lana carried her coat, probably the only reason she wasn't sweating from sprinting through three concourses. The other agent miraculously appeared free, which was never a good sign. Travelers always needed something. *Please let me not have run all this way and be hyperventilating for nothing.* Lana sent a prayer to the heavens and pushed forward.

~o~

The first thing Edmund Clayton III noticed was her legs. Which made him a total cad, he knew. His mother had definitely raised him better. But, as if he'd been captured by the pull of a powerful electromagnet, his gaze followed endless, sheer black tights upward, from their start in black suede boots until the silky fabric disappeared beneath a red and green corduroy tartan hem that skimmed mid-thigh. He rationalized that he couldn't help but stare—the woman had made quite the entrance by approaching the service desk like a mini-tornado. Her chest heaved and her boots clicked on the worn linoleum while her four-wheeled, hard-side carry-on whirred in its attempt to keep up the frantic pace. As she came alongside him at the service desk, her bag rolled over his left foot.

"Sorry." She gasped out the word as she spared him one those automatic, yet polite, apologetic smiles strangers give one another. Still somewhat breathless, the words gushed out. "I need to get on this plane." She shoved her phone forward, her boarding pass visible as she shoved her arm toward the gate agent. "It's not full yet, is it?"

Without waiting for an answer, she leaned over the counter, the interesting gap forming under the top button of her red silk shirt revealing a peek of black lace. "Please, tell me you have a seat."

The agent offered a "Let me check" and then a "Yes. I can make the change."

A husky, still-catching-her-breath voice conveyed relief. "Thank you. Whatever it is, I'll take it."

As she stopped leaning and straightened, her soft shoulder bag slipped. Whatever hard object was inside smacked his funny bone with a thwack. He grimaced, and her wide-eyed amber gaze caught his over the bottle of water she was sipping. She readjusted her shoulder strap and shoved the bottle into a side pocket. "I'm so sorry."

"Sir?" the gate agent asked. Edmund's attention snapped back to the representative helping him. "This is the best I can do. I'm sorry we didn't have anything better. But at least it's not the middle of the last row."

"Which I appreciate." He fingered the paper-thin boarding pass and checked his frustration. He could do this stupid undercover week. Even if it meant the VP of Clayton Hotels flew coach class rather than on his private plane. What was four hours plus a two-time zone change on a commercial carrier in the grand scheme of things if it meant beating Reginald Justus? Peanuts. A minor inconvenience. A small price to pay to own Van Horn hotels and add them to the Clayton Holdings portfolio.

Thankfully Edmund hadn't had to wear his ridiculous Peter Waggoner costume on the flight. The mouth partial that changed Edmund's voice took several minutes to adhere. Then there was the rest of his disguise...

Her bag clipped his arm again, and her lips puckered into a perfect pink O that sent a jolt through him. She looped the strap back onto her shoulder. "Sorry. I don't know what's gotten into this thing today."

"It's fine." Edmund uttered some of the most meaningless words in the English language. He stepped away, but not before committing her to memory, same as he'd do with any guest or business associate. Sizing someone up and filing information away was ingrained habit. Good business acumen. A way to stay one step ahead. A winning tactic. Never mind the fact that he found her interesting, despite her lack of control over her luggage. She was pretty too, in that natural, fresh-faced way.

Her skin rivaled milk. A light smattering of freckles graced a perky petite nose. He had a Roman nose: the same one his father had, and his grandfather, and his brothers Michael and Liam. It was something the show's producers had argued over how to hide, and since the onsite producer was going to be Lachlan Van Horn himself, Edmund had sided with whatever Lachlan wanted. In the end, they'd decided to make it larger, meaning Edmund would have to glue a prosthetic to his face every morning.

Lachlan, who'd also serve as director, had suggested getting into character immediately, but Edmund had pushed back on that. While Edmund would forgo the company plane and fly coach, he'd drawn the line at traveling as Peter. Oh, and no way was Edmund sitting in the row directly in front of the aft lavatory. A man of his stature had his limits. Bad enough he had to settle onto one of those too small chairs lining the gate. After trying and failing to make himself comfortable, Edmund sent his younger sister a text: "I'm traveling coach."

Seconds later Eva replied, "All part of being a common man" and punctuated her text with a laughing emoji. The baby in the family, she took liberties like that.

Unamused, Edmund sent back the vomit emoji. He didn't care if the action was childish or churlish. He considered his Gulfstream an extension of his office. A place to work and get things done. Instead, he languished in the waiting area along with the general public while the clock ticked away the wasted minutes. He studied the crowd, his gaze again landing on the woman at the counter before he received two more laughing faces from Eva and a "You'll beat Justus. You'll wow 'em." His phone pinged with an additional text: "You'll do great. When don't you?"

He appreciated Eva's confidence. She'd told him Reginald Justus had already completed his undercover week at one of his Florida adventure resorts. Until she had shared that news, Edmund had held out hope that Justus would back out of the wager. Since he hadn't, Edmund was locked into completing his week. Both his father and uncle had loved the undercover idea, not that they'd ever consider doing one themselves.

As for the show, once it aired, as the company's VP of PR, Eva planned to use the program as the capstone for her latest social media and advertising campaign. "Think of it as a working vacation. Like going to camp," she'd told Edmund as he'd packed his suitcase. "How hard can performing various hotel jobs be?"

Edmund would soon find out. He stretched tense fingers and shifted on the hard plastic. He hated reality TV, hated gossip. Thankfully no one took notice of him, which allowed him to relax somewhat. In hindsight, dating a popular social media influencer had not been one of his best ideas. But when he'd first met Veronica, she'd seemed perfect. Sweet. Kind. He simply hadn't realized until too late that she'd been two different people—the pretty popular girl in public and in private, the insecure, high maintenance woman worried about her numbers, clicks, and having Edmund's entire attention.

Despite this, he'd tried to make the relationship work, including asking her to marry him. He'd realized now he'd been unable to wrap his brain around the fact that he couldn't fix things and make them better. Marriage should make her more secure, right?

Once the veneer came off, all they did was fight. Then Veronica had asked him to dinner. Had he known the video of Veronica tossing his ring at him over crème brulee would be number one over video of an imploding pop star, Edmund never would have agreed to meet. Count trusting Veronica as one of his biggest mistakes.

A harried gate agent announced Edmund's boarding group, and because Edmund refused to lose even more pride by failing to land Van Horn hotels, he joined the queue and shuffled his way down the jet bridge. He stowed his luggage and folded his six-foot bulk into seat 10A, sighing as his knees touched the seatback in front of him.

"I see we both got seats," a familiar voice said. Shoulder length hair the color of sunset swished as she opened the overhead bin. The tan silk inched upward, providing a tantalizing view of the pinky-sized dip of her bellybutton. She handed him the overcoat he'd stowed. "Hold that a second, will you? I need to make this fit."

Her shirt climbed further, exposing a good three inches of creamy skin as she shoved her suitcase overhead. She replaced his coat, clicked the bin closed, and dropped into the aisle seat. Edmund pressed against the window as her deadly, smaller matching tote came close to taking out his arm.

"Sorry." The tote wobbled in her lap, her bottom gyrating as she withdrew a paperback novel, a bottle of water smaller than the one he'd carried on, and a yellow package of peanut M&M's. She shoved the tote under the seat and extended her right hand, the gape at the V of her breasts providing clear confirmation of black lace. "How about we start over? I'm Lana."

Coming soon in 2024 from Harlequin Special Edition

Acknowledgments

For my fans, who've stayed with me for 20 years, and for my own daughters, who mean the world. While places in the book are real, they've been fictionalized and are in no means representative of real people or circumstances.

About the Author

Describing herself as a woman who does way too much and never wants to stop, Michele Dunaway is a bestselling author and award-winning high school English teacher. Proud mother of two daughters, Michele is an avid pet lover who shares her home with far too many rescued cats, who of course completely rule the roost.